PRAISE FOR THE FIERY TALES

"Wickedly passionate . . . [A] sensual treat!"
—Sylvia Day,
#1 *New York Times* bestselling author

"Hot enough to warm the coldest winter night."
—Publishers Weekly

"Lushly erotic . . . Sophisticated and deeply romantic."
—Elizabeth Hoyt,
New York Times bestselling author

"Sure to delight!"
—Jennifer Ashley,
New York Times bestselling author

"The most luscious, sexy take on classic fairy tales I've ever read!"
—Cheryl Holt,
New York Times bestselling author

The Duke's Match Girl

A Christmas Fiery Tale

LILA DIPASQUA

DiPasqua

Copyright © 2013 by Lila DiPasqua
Cover design by Lila DiPasqua, Bruno DiPasqua, and Seductive Designs
Interior Design by Woven Red Author Services, www.WovenRed.ca
Edited by Linda Ingmanson

ISBN: 978-0-9880350-3-4 (trade pbk)
ISBN: 978-0-9880350-2-7(e-book)

To everyone who's ever been given a second chance at love.
And to those who gave it to them.

To the real life Leo—one of the strongest men I've ever met.

To my awesome street team, The Pavement Princesses,
who are like royalty to me.

And as always, to the loves of my heart—
Carm and my three angels.

Finally, to God. He knows why.

A Historical Tidbit

DO YOU KNOW WHEN fairy tales were born? It was not so long ago. During the reign of King Louis XIV. His court was as decadent as it was opulent. A time of high culture, elegance, and excesses. The pursuit of sinful pleasures was a pastime. Sex, an art form. You see, Louis was a lusty king. He and his courtiers were connoisseurs of the carnal arts.

It was during this wickedly wonderful time that author Charles Perrault (creator of *The Tales of Mother Goose*) first began writing down fairy tales—the folklore that had been passed on verbally for generations. It wasn't long before fairy tales became a highly fashionable topic of discussion in the renowned salons of Paris. Though the fairy tale *The Little Match Girl* (1845) was made famous by Hans Christian Andersen, a Danish poet and author, perhaps his muse was stirred by hearing about characters such as these…

[NOTE: Though more inexpensive, self-igniting matchsticks weren't invented until the 1800s, there were earlier cruder versions of the modern-day match created by a number of inventors in the 17th century. In 17th century France, there were many independent, self-reliant women, many of whom were making a lucrative living at writing the popular genre of fairy tales. I see no reason not to believe that a bright young woman could have been the first inventor of the matchstick… And whose name may have simply fallen through the cracks of time.]

CHAPTER ONE

"Once in a while, right in the middle of an ordinary life,
love gives us a fairy tale."
~ Anonymous

December, 1685
France

"LEO, YOU ARE up to something. Out with it." Daniel sported his usual smile, his arm draped casually over the back of the damask chair he occupied.

Chuckling softly, Bernard sauntered over to the ebony side table and poured himself a fresh brandy from the decanter. The sound of the amber liquid draining into his crystal goblet mingled with the crackling fire in the hearth. "It's a new mistress, isn't it, Leo? Come now. Give us the details. *Dieu*. Do you ever give that prick of yours a rest?"

Leopold Charles Nicolas d'Ermart, Duc de Mont-Marly, ignored the comment.

As well as the burst of mirth it inspired from his two younger brothers.

Bracing his shoulder against the window frame, he crossed his arms and gazed outside at the vast grounds of Montbrison, lightly dusted with snow.

If only it were merely a new conquest.

The urge to glance at the clock on the mantel seized hold of him.

Again.

The ticking had started to grate on him, its incessant sound far more difficult to ignore than the needling from his siblings.

Where the bloody hell is Gilles? His man should have returned with a response to Leo's offer by now. The anticipation was driving him utterly mad.

He wasn't accustomed to waiting for things, yet he'd waited for this opportunity—this moment—hell, this one woman for years.

This was one seduction he was pursuing with slow, methodical steps.

If things went as planned, Leo wasn't going to be able to hide what he was truly up to from his brothers. Nor did he care to.

His plan was centered on Suzanne Matchet. So unlike any woman he'd ever known—and he'd known her forever.

Full of adorable little quirks and oddities. With big, alluring brown eyes. A brilliant mind for science. And the only woman in the realm who preferred he fall off a cliff.

And for a damned good reason, too.

"Now, Bernard," Daniel said. "I'm sure there's a woman or two left whom our brother hasn't sampled." He grinned.

Leo frowned and grappled with his patience. Normally, he was unfazed by his brothers' baiting and ribbing. But today he was on edge. "Are you both quite done?"

"Not until you tell us who she is," Bernard said.

Daniel was quick to add, "And how delicious she is."

They were now both sporting the same idiotic grin.

It took everything inside him not to punch the wall. Something, *anything* to vent the frustration mountaining inside him as he waited.

And waited.

And, *Jésus-Christ*, waited some more.

What was taking Gilles so fucking long? He should have been

engaged in a private meeting with Gilles right at this very moment, rather than this grating conversation with Daniel and Bernard.

Though Leo and his brothers kept little from each other, Suzanne was not a subject he'd ever discussed with them. That wasn't because he *didn't* know how delicious she was.

In truth, he did. He knew every last mouthwatering inch of her.

He knew more than just her body and the sweet spots that made her melt and moan for him. He knew her deepest secrets. Her hopes and dreams. The sweet way she'd tug on her ear whenever she was nervous or deep in thought. And the way she'd tangle a finger in one of her silky curls and absently play with the strand when she was engrossed in a book. Though he hadn't laid eyes on her in years, he could effortlessly recall that little crinkle that would form on her brow whenever a pensive expression shaped her comely features.

Christ, he could effortlessly recall countless memories of her.

And he was sick and tired of battling them back.

She was ten years of age when first she came to live at Château Montbrison with her father, then the newly appointed official physician of the d'Ermart family.

Leo was twelve.

He'd been immediately taken aback by the pretty, spirited girl who had marched straight up to him upon their first introduction, flouting convention and forgetting her place, despite her father's gentle admonishment. She had a habit of speaking to Leo with a bluntness no one else ever dared use. She'd never placated him simply because he was the heir to a duchy. Or to win favor, as others did. And she could climb a tree—all while in skirts—as fast as he and his brothers. Always eager to prove she was just as clever and brave as any boy.

They became instant allies, and friends.

A smile tugged hard at the corners of Leo's mouth as their childhood mischief flitted through his mind. He and Suzanne were constantly aggravating the servants. Peeping over countertops, they'd snatch food off the trays, food meant for his parents or guests—just for the fun of it—then race off into the extensive gardens at Montbrison for private picnics. He'd spent hours lying beside her on the grass staring up at the sky, utterly charmed and entertained as he listened to the random scientific facts she'd relay—whatever happen to manifest at that moment in her bright mind. She had devoured the books in her father's personal library voraciously. And those in the large library at Montbrison.

Normally, prattle about science would have bored him beyond measure.

But there was absolutely nothing boring about the very unique Suzanne Matchet.

And on one Christmas Eve—eight years after they first met—their relationship progressed from the best of friends...

To lovers.

"Will you look at him, Daniel?" Bernard said, motioning to Leo with a jerk of his chin. "He's practically smiling. The sex must be excellent."

Daniel strolled over to Bernard and propped his elbow on Bernard's shoulder. "Yes, and he still has not shared the tantalizing tidbits."

Oh, there were definitely *tantalizing tidbits*.

And *excellent* wasn't a strong enough word to accurately describe what had transpired between them that extraordinary night.

She'd tasted so good. She'd felt incredible; he couldn't get enough of the delectable clench of her hot, silky sex squeezing around his thrusting prick. And those exquisite little spasms of her vaginal walls rippling down his length as she came on his cock were nothing short of mind-melting.

But that wasn't all.

The physical ecstasy wasn't the only thing that had made the sexual experience so astounding.

It was the emotions that he hadn't felt before—or since—during sex.

At a time when he'd normally be reveling in pure lust, he'd been inundated with soft emotions, intensifying the encounter in ways he'd never anticipated. Heightening the hunger. And spiking each and every sensation that swamped his body.

It was the most unforgettable experience of his life.

And Lord knew he'd done everything in his power to forget it—and her.

He'd spent the last seven years drowning himself in every vice just to purge her from his system.

And failed miserably.

He didn't know when the exact moment was, when precisely it happened. But somewhere along the way, she'd stolen his heart.

Years later, he was still reeling.

He'd had no right to make promises he couldn't keep just to have her. He'd fought the sexual pull that had been mounting fiercely over time as hard as he could. *Merde*, he'd even left Montbrison for several months, staying at his family's hôtel in Paris hoping to snap the allure.

It didn't work.

The moment he returned, the attraction between them ignited into an inferno once more. The air practically crackled with the fire that burned between them. It was so deliciously hot. So completely untamable. He found himself having to control his breathing and his gaze around her so he wasn't gawking at her. Or panting like a bloody dog. It didn't help that he'd stolen a kiss before he left for Paris. The memory of that kiss burned in his mind and body the entire time he'd been away.

He returned famished for another taste.

Worse, he was still just as ravenous today.

Leo cast a sidelong glance at his brothers. "Don't the two of you have something better to do today than annoy me? Have another brandy. Play some Basset. Perhaps take a walk off a cliff?"

They burst into good-natured laughter, not in the least bit offended.

Daniel shook his head. "I cannot believe our brother isn't sharing with us, Bernard."

"Yes, and I'm quite wounded by it." Bernard placed a hand over his chest as if pained.

Bernard had no idea what wounded felt like. Neither had he, until the morning after their night together, that Christmas Day, when everything imploded. The look of devastation on her lovely face still tormented him. The very next day, Suzanne's father, Richard Matchet, respectfully resigned his post and left with his brokenhearted daughter.

She was gone from Leo's life. For good. In an instant.

For months he walked around feeling winded, as though someone had slammed him in the chest.

Two months later, Leo learned Suzanne's father had become the town doctor in Maillard, attending to those less fortunate. Barely scraping by. He'd traded the opulence of his private apartments in Château Montbrison, with a personal staff to attend to him and his daughter, for a humble hovel.

And that tormented Leo, too.

After all this time, she still lingered on the fringes of his mind and made appearances in more erotic dreams than he could comfortably count.

There were too many things left unsaid.

There were too many unresolved emotions and desires that ran so deep, they'd become imprinted on his very marrow.

He'd no idea if the connection they'd once shared still existed. Or if it would even be possible to recapture even a fraction of what had slipped through his fingers. But he had to try.

Or he'd never have a moment of mental peace.

Nor vanquish the ache in his gut that hadn't abated since the day she left.

Dieu, was she going to accept his offer? Leo glanced at the clock, unable to help himself. Only five minutes had passed since the last time he looked.

And still no Gilles. *Fuck*.

"You'll survive, Bernard." He managed to keep his tone bland, belying the tension inside him.

"Can you at least tell us why in the world there is such a flurry of activity among the servants?" Bernard pressed. "And they are all quite tight-lipped about it, too."

"They have been attending to your needs during your visit, and they are preparing for the arrivals of Elisabeth and Aurore." Not exactly the whole truth. But that was all Bernard was going to get for now. It was a believable partial truth. Christmas was in a mere ten days. The balance of Leo's siblings would be arriving soon.

But none of that was going to be a hindrance to his objective—getting Suzanne back under his roof.

He never expected to see his brown-eyed beauty again.

He certainly never expected his life to take the shocking turn it had four months ago.

His disastrous marriage to Constance had come to an abrupt end. Her sensational death brought to light her affair with the Marquis de Chermont and set the gossipmongers' tongues wagging in every salon in Paris.

He didn't care a whit what people had to say.

He'd known of Constance's extramarital indulgence with Chermont for a long time—or at least suspected as much. Leo hadn't lived under the same roof as his wife for years.

Not since the night they'd consummated the marriage. He'd been gentle with his bride, even while he had a heavy heart and could still taste Suzanne's lips. Still remember the feel of her skin. All the while plagued by the fact that Suzanne had been the last woman he'd kissed. Touched. Had. And the only woman he'd hungered for then…and ever since.

After the deed was done, he'd found himself with a weeping wife on his hands.

Not exactly the sort of reaction he'd ever experienced after sex.

It had taken some coaxing, but he finally learned the truth behind Constance's tears. She had been in love with Chermont since girlhood. Her father had refused to consider the match, opting for a future duc for his daughter. Instead of a marquis.

Constance's words had turned the lingering ache in his chest to a sharp stab.

Her circumstance was far too familiar and resonated deep inside him.

He'd done what was required of him. He'd married the woman he'd been expected to wed to increase his family's already vast wealth and further advance their political power.

But he'd be damned if he was going to force a woman into his bed who longed for another.

The entire situation was nothing but a stinging reminder of his own deplorable predicament. And what—or rather whom—he'd personally given up in the name of duty.

Leo left for Paris that night, much to Constance's relief, no doubt, and never lived under the same roof with her again.

Though he'd never wished her dead, the plain fact was that he was a widower.

And now he was free.

Free to pursue what been left unfinished. Since learning from Gilles of Richard Matchet's passing, knowing Suzanne was alone in the world and surviving on the coins she made as an apothecary, he was even more eager to bring her back to Montbrison.

The timing was finally right. And he was going after this—after *her*—with a vengeance.

All he needed now was favorable news from Gilles.

"Your Grace?" His servant's voice grabbed Leo's attention. At the doorway of the room stood somber-faced Isaac. An elderly, tall, thin man, Isaac had been in service to his family since Leo could remember. "My lords." Isaac bowed to Bernard and Daniel before promptly returning his attention to Leo. "Monsieur Gilles awaits you in your private apartments, Your Grace."

Leo was already stalking out of the room before Isaac had finished his sentence. At a brisk pace, he exited the study, crossed the large vestibule, and climbed the stairs two at a time, arriving on the second floor in the east wing in no time.

Throwing open the door to his private rooms, he found Gilles seated in one of the upholstered chairs near the hearth in the antechamber.

Gilles came to his feet in a quick, fluid motion, despite his stocky build.

Upon seeing his man standing there, knowing he had news at last, Leo was hit with a sudden uncharacteristic pang of uncertainty. *What if this is a mistake?* Perhaps he should have left well enough alone.

Seven years was a long time. People changed.

Suzanne might not be the same person he'd once known. She might be nothing like the woman he craved.

Shoving aside his doubts, he said, "It's about time. What news have you? Did the lady respond to the offer?"

Gilles's full cheeks reddened slightly, and he adjusted the cravat around his thick neck. "Yes, Your Grace, she did."

Leo placed his hands on his hips, wrestling with his patience. "*Well?*" *Dieu.* Was he going to have to drag each word out of him? Last night, his dream of Suzanne had been so vivid, he could actually taste her soft mouth, and feel the luscious texture of her skin.

He woke up with his cock as stiff as a spike. Longing for her even more fiercely.

"What did she say? I want to know—*word for word*," he demanded.

Gilles cleared his throat. A small bead of sweat appeared on his forehead. "Of course, Your Grace." He couldn't have looked more uneasy. Leo had never seen his loyal, ever-competent man so discomposed. "I know how important it is to provide you with an accurate account of her response. And, well, she… You see… She…"

"*Yes?* Out with it!" *Jésus-Christ. How bloody difficult is this?*

"Your Grace, I-I don't think that… What I mean to say is, I don't believe I can put it to you, sir, quite the way she did."

"Why the hell not?"

Gilles quickly reached inside his dark green justacorps and pulled out a note from the pocket of the knee-length coat. "Upon hearing her response, I thought it best that she impart her message to you in a note. She wholeheartedly agreed. This is what she said, word for word, just as you requested." He held out the note to him.

Leo snatched it from his hand and unfolded it in an instant.

For the first time in a long time, he was staring at Suzanne Matchet's distinct handwriting. His eyes quickly scanned her words.

Your Grace,

Your man has informed me of your offer. He was quite uncomfortable about relaying my response. It is for his ease that I put it to you here in writing. As to your offer—and I say this with the utmost sincerity—you may take it, and insert it into your exalted posterior.

Sincerely,
Suzanne

Leo's gaze shot from the note to Gilles. His man was now blushing profusely, his discomfort coming off him in palpable waves. Glancing back down at the words scribed before him, Leo felt the beginnings of a smile pulling hard at the corners of his mouth. He burst into laughter, the sudden jovial sound making poor Gilles jump.

Leo clamped a hand on Gilles's shoulder. "You've done well." He couldn't contain his grin.

Gilles looked utterly stunned. "*I have?*"

"Indeed. I'll take it from here."

Leo walked out still grinning, the note still in hand.

Gilles's visit to Suzanne had garnered for Leo all the

information he wished to know. Suzanne hadn't changed. Not one bit. She was still the same feisty, beautiful girl he'd let slip through his fingers.

He wanted her back in his life. And in his bed. Having mastered the art of seduction long ago, he'd seduced her once, claiming her innocence and ultimately breaking her heart in the process. But he was the one who was different now.

And this time, things were going to be different.

This time, he was going to show her the depth of his desire.

This time, he wasn't about to let her get away.

CHAPTER TWO

"A CHICKEN?" Lucille's brow furrowed with her dismay, deepening the grooves on her aged face. "That's what she paid you? A *chicken?*"

"Now, Lucille, don't badger Suzanne," scolded Rosalie, Lucille's sister, always quick to come to Suzanne's defense. Rosalie set a bowl on the long wooden table before her sister. "Focus on crumbling the mint."

Suzanne calmly walked past the two older women in her employ as they stood near the floor-to-ceiling shelves of spices, herbs, and dried roots that ran the length of one of the walls in her apothecary shop. She knew Rosalie was trying to distract Lucille by suggesting a task that would keep her busy.

A futile endeavor.

Nothing actually distracted Lucille from offering up her opinion. On everything.

Repeatedly.

Though Suzanne had come to adore the opinionated woman over the years, Lucille could be trying at times.

Suzanne stooped to give an affectionate pat to Gaspard, her gray cat. Lying in his favorite spot near the fire, he stretched lazily with an approving purr. "That was merely a gift. Madame Dubois assures me she will have the funds by tomorrow, Lucille. I wasn't going to deny her young son the nutmeg oil he needed for his stomach ailment."

"Yes. Yes. She's quite right, sister," Rosalie said. "She can hardly deny a sick child." She shoved Lucille's bowl of mint, still untouched, closer to Lucille, trying to encourage her to start working.

Lucille simply ignored it. "You wouldn't have to worry about coin if you had accepted the duc's offer."

A streak of cold anger shot down Suzanne's spine. A purely reflexive response at the mention of *Leo*. The arrogant aristo who thought he could snap his fingers and she'd come running—after all these years—to do his bidding, with no regard whatsoever for all the hurt he'd caused.

Apparently, the mighty Leo d'Ermart simply woke up one morning and decided to reappear in her life, bold as could be— and sent his personal secretary to deliver his offer, no less.

How very thoughtful.

The man's gall was outrageous.

Tamping down her ire, she gave Gaspard another pat. He purred contently. "I'm not worried about coin. There's no need to be." Suzanne cast Lucille a reassuring smile over her shoulder. Since her father's death, she'd managed just fine.

"But… But…I just don't understand it," Lucille continued, unrelenting. "He has plenty of wealth. You make concoctions for so many others. Why not make the perfumes he's requesting? He is willing to pay a vast sum. An offer from a duc does not come around every day!"

Because his offer is nothing but a ruse.

She was no fool. The generous funds Leo was offering her to create perfumes for his two sisters—meant to be gifts—had a condition: she was to come to Montbrison to create them.

The offer was bogus. A mere pretense to get her to his château.

She wanted nothing more to do with him.

Knowing the unscrupulous rake as well as she did, his true motives were without a doubt of a disreputable nature. She refused to be duped by his little ploy. She'd experienced his stinging trickery before.

It had taken a long time for her heart to mend and harden against Leo d'Ermart. It had been years before she'd finally managed to wrestle him out of her daily thoughts. And heart. She resented it that yesterday he'd intruded into her mental peace once more—thanks to Gilles's visit.

The best thing a woman could do was to stay far away from the notorious roué.

And that was exactly what she intended to do.

She rose, firmly shoving all thoughts of Leo from her mind.

Over the fire simmered a concoction of juice from unripe poppies and herbs. She gave it a gentle stir. It was a remedy for nervousness and insomnia she was preparing for the blacksmith's wife, Madame Clavel, who swore by Suzanne's elixir. Science had always fascinated her. It was one of her greatest passions. Though, as a woman, Suzanne knew she could never be a member of the Royal Academy of Sciences.

But that didn't stop her from striving to know more than the men who were—thanks to her father who'd encouraged rather than discouraged her thirst for knowledge. He was simply a brilliant physician who'd understood her need to feed her mind.

He wasn't like the other private physicians who tended to the aristocracy.

Her father disliked their conventional treatments. Especially bloodlettings and purgatives. He'd noted long ago that the lower classes' more natural, less invasive remedies had a far better success rate.

And he'd adopted those treatments in his practice early on.

She had him to thank for her interest in scientific experiments and her knowledge of the healing properties of plants. Knowledge she'd expanded on, improving many of his treatments.

Much to his pride and delight.

"But he's a *duc*..." Lucille was still lamenting. "I've never seen you turn away anyone who requested your services. Why turn him away?"

The subject of Leo d'Ermart was far too emotional and not

one she was going to discuss with Lucille. Or anyone. Nor was she going to admit to just how much satisfaction she'd derived from writing Leo that note. The man deserved to be knocked off his perch. It felt good to be the woman to do so.

His comeuppance was long overdue.

She'd dealt with the matter. And she was glad to be rid of him.

For good.

"Lucille, I've made my decision. Do leave the matter be." She felt confident that the sale of her medicines and perfumes would be more than adequate to see her through the winter. Moreover, her newest scientific advancement had worked wonders. A stick dipped in sulfur and one dipped in phosphorous, when struck against one another, created a flame. She'd begun selling her matchsticks four days ago with some success already.

A further boost to her funds.

If only her father had been around to see this latest scientific achievement. What she wouldn't give to have him there for just one more Christmas. As it was, she dreaded the upcoming fête. It would be hollow and empty, her first without him.

His death had left a profound ache in her heart, as intense as the pain she'd felt over Leo years ago.

She didn't need to add to her grief by reopening old wounds.

Discouraging Leo had been the right thing to do. The highhanded aristo had no place in her life anymore.

Lucille threw up her hands and finally began crumbling the dried mint in the bowl. "Who refuses a *duc*?" she muttered.

Therein was the core of the problem. Seven years ago, Suzanne hadn't refused him, fool that she was.

And look how badly that turned out for you.

"Now, sister." Rosalie swiped a strand of salt-and-pepper hair off her forehead. "If Suzanne doesn't wish to take coin from some old potbellied duc, then that is her choice to make."

Suzanne gave the concoction another stir as the image of a paunchy Leo d'Ermart formed in her mind's eye.

Wouldn't that be poetic justice?

Unfortunately, the mere presence of a potbelly would be no deterrent to the females who flocked to him. His extraordinary wealth and power was like an aphrodisiac. He'd still draw female attention everywhere he went. And he had been busy. Last year, one of her father's patients had brought her a number of copies of the various Paris papers to enjoy. Leo's conquests had made plenty of fodder for the gossip sheets.

A sudden clattering of horses' hooves against cobblestones grabbed her attention. The sound rose quickly, getting louder with its rapid approach, obliterating the din of the townspeople moving about on foot and in carts outside.

This was a team of horses.

A large one.

A team of horses that had just come to an abrupt stop directly on the other side of her shop's door.

Suzanne tensed, unable to shake the sudden dread that crested over her. Deep in the pit of her belly, she was gripped by a strong, unshakeable feeling that she knew exactly who had just arrived. Large teams of horses were not an everyday occurrence in Maillard.

No. Impossible… She'd unequivocally rebuffed Leo.

It couldn't be him. Could it?

Lucille bolted for the window before Suzanne could stop her. "There's a carriage with six horses here!" she all but squealed. "That's a *DUC!*"

Rosalie wasted no time darting to her sibling's side. She let out her own shriek of excitement. "There are definitely six horses. It *is* a duc! *Oh, my…* I believe he's coming this way!"

The door suddenly opened.

Suzanne's stomach dropped.

Three large men—including Gilles—entered her shop, one by one bowing to her briefly. Just as the third stepped to one side, a gust of winter wind stole into the room.

Suzanne barely felt the chill. She was far too stunned by the presence of the tall, familiar form now filling her doorway. And the breathtaking changes in him that had taken place these last seven years. *Gracious God…*

A second breeze wafted in, ruffling the hem of Leo's long black cloak. Caressing his dark hair.

Against her will, she took in the breadth of his shoulders, which were wider, even more powerful, his handsome face that was more mature.

And more devastating.

Everything about him had seemingly intensified, from the hardness of his chiseled body to the hue of those spellbinding light green eyes. He had a presence and air of authority like never before.

Before her stood an incredibly gorgeous male who completely dominated the room. *One who's caused you more pain than anyone else ever has in your life.*

And he was more attractive than ever.

Good Lord. There *was* no justice. There wasn't the slightest hint of a potbelly on that flat, firm abdomen.

Realizing she was gawking at him, she quickly yanked her gaze back up. The moment she met his seductive eyes, a slow smile formed on his lips. He'd caught her ogling him. Suzanne blushed, unladylike expletives blaring in her head. The very ones she'd learned in childhood following the d'Ermart brothers around their vast estate.

That's just perfect. He is arrogant enough, and you've just fed his conceit further by openly gaping at him.

He approached, a casual, all-too-confident advance, then stopped directly in front of her, still sporting his beautiful half smile.

He was even more glorious up close.

"Hello, Suzanne." His voice had the same deep, rich sound. Its effect was like warm nectar poured over chilled skin. She quashed the shiver that quivered down her spine—immediately irked at herself for allowing even the slightest reaction to his male beauty.

It's that very same masculine beauty and charm that was your downfall.

She'd learned not to trust that handsome face. Or any man

whose eyes always shone with wicked promise.

"It is wonderful to see you again," he said.

A slight gasp caught her attention. It came from Rosalie. Or perhaps it was Lucille. The two sisters stood side by side, mouths fully agape, their gazes darting from Leo, to her, and back to Leo once more.

Rosalie was the first to clamp her mouth shut. She poked her sister in the ribs. "*He knows our Suzanne,*" she said in a loud whisper. A big, beaming smile formed on her face. "*And he's happy to see her again. Isn't that delightful, sister?*"

Lucille frowned. "*I'm not deaf, Rosalie. I heard him perfectly well.*" Lucille's whisper was just as elevated as her sibling's was, reaching everyone in the room, including those from Leo's entourage—if their glances at her elderly employees were any indication. "*What I'd like to know is where does he know her from?*"

"Rosalie, Lucille, please…" she reprimanded gently. This was bad enough without their commentary.

Amusement shone in Leo's eyes, but he remained silent. Clearly, he'd discerned instantly that the women were hopelessly imprudent busybodies.

"My father was the personal physician to the duc and his family once." There. Hopefully that would hush them for a moment or two.

"Oh, was he?" Lucille's brows shot up, looking quite elated by this news.

Rosalie's reaction was entirely different. At the mention of Suzanne's father, Rosalie burst into an audible sob. She fished out a handkerchief from her bodice, wiped her tears, then blew her nose loudly before composing herself. "God rest him… That dear, dear man…"

"He was indeed a fine man," Leo concurred without taking his eyes off Suzanne. "Your father shall be greatly missed by all who knew him."

Suzanne felt the tears rush to her eyes and quickly blinked them back. She wasn't going to cry before Leo and his men. She was stronger than that. She kept her pain private, confined to the silent tears she shed on her pillow on those rare nights when she let herself cry.

"Thank you," she managed to say, forcing the words up her constricted throat, a little unbalanced by his remarks. Since leaving Montbrison, she'd continued to correspond with Leo's sisters. She utterly adored Aurore and Elisabeth. They visited her and her father from time to time, and treated her like sister. They were so different from their eldest brother. There wasn't a deceptive bone in their bodies. Suzanne knew Aurore and Elisabeth had informed the rest of their siblings of her father's death. She'd received letters of condolence from each of the d'Ermart brothers.

Except Leo.

And she was rather glad about that. Grateful, in fact, that she'd been spared any dealings with Leo d'Ermart—until Gilles showed up on her doorstep with Leo's offer.

She hadn't expected to see Leo ever again. And now she was under the unnerving scrutiny of those sensuous light-colored eyes as they gazed at her boldly. With a certain unmistakable heat.

Oh, she knew that look.

That look meant trouble.

For her.

For any woman who was on the receiving end of one of Leo's smoldering gazes.

That same undercurrent of desire she'd once felt from him was still there.

That unsettled her further. Clearly, she was right about him. His motives *were* merely carnal in nature. He'd been a force to contend with—utterly irresistible—seven years ago when he was younger. Less experienced at seduction.

She certainly didn't want to take on the now highly potent master seducer, the Duc de Mont-Marly. They'd competed against each other many times as children. But this wasn't a childish game. Under no circumstances was she going to fall victim to this dangerously attractive man's charms.

Not ever again.

Suzanne clasped her hands, then unclasped them, feeling beyond awkward, when she'd always prided herself on being confident and undaunted in any situation. Leo was rattling her, making her tense. And nervous. Dear God. She could feel another trying blush heating her cheeks, and she had no idea why she was blushing this much. She wanted to kick herself. She hadn't blushed in the longest time. This was certainly no time to begin anew.

And because she was under Leo's intense regard, he had definitely noticed.

Moreover, there was little doubt that Lucille and Rosalie had noticed, too. Their curiosity about her and the duc was mounting by the moment. There'd be no peace once he left. They were going to assail her with questions.

She took in a quiet, fortifying breath, ignoring his wonderful scent. It was one of the many things that used to draw her to him and ultimately lured her to her ruin.

The sooner he left, the better.

"Your Grace…" She purposely addressed him formally rather than with the usual more familiar manner she'd always used in the past. Formality kept a distance between them, and that was exactly what she wanted. Actually, what she wanted was for Leo d'Ermart to be back at Montbrison. Or in Paris. Or any place that was far away and not threatening to add to her emotional turmoil. "I pray your visit to my humble shop isn't due to your offer. I sent a note with your man. Did you not receive it?" she asked pointedly, holding his gaze firmly, despite her disquiet. It was more than a mere question.

It was a purposeful reminder of her rebuke over his lascivious intentions.

She wanted him to know she wasn't fooled by his veiled excuse to entice her to his château. There weren't many that would have refused him. In fact, not a single soul in the realm. And certainly no one would have dared write a note, such as the one she did, to any member of his powerful family.

Especially to the Duc de Mont-Marly himself.

But she wasn't intimidated by Leo. Never had been. It was the first time she'd ever scribed an impolite letter. But the libertine deserved it—and he needed to be discouraged.

She readied herself for his response. Let him be angry or insulted. Or both. It didn't matter. She was sending the rake—and his deceptive ways—straight back to whence he came.

But to her amazement, Leo didn't comment at all.

Instead, he turned and sauntered away and began a slow perusal of her shop, leisurely taking in its details, pulling the occasional jar off a shelf to investigate its contents.

Appearing quite engrossed and unconcerned.

Just how long was she going to have to watch him survey her herbs and instruments? Seeing him move about the room, all that riveting male perfection and masculine grace, was maddening.

She glanced at Gilles, unsure what to make of his master's reaction. Gilles shifted his weight, yet said nothing.

Stopping at the table with the mint, Leo picked up the bowl with the crumbled herb, took a casual sniff, and set it back down.

It was then that he finally met her gaze.

"Yes, Suzanne, I got your note," he said at last, his tone mild.

That was it? That was the sum of his reaction to the contents of her note? No irritation? Or vexation?

Nothing?

She glanced back at Gilles. His gaze immediately shot down, and he feigned interest with something on the floor. He was well aware of what she wrote to his master. *His* disquiet was evident.

But not Leo. He'd resumed his browsing of her shop with a casual comfort.

"*And?*" she prompted, feeling ruffled, her nerves taut as her words to him still hung in the air. Unanswered. For goodness sake, she'd indelicately told him where to stick his offer. Wasn't he going to say *something* about it?

He stopped, having finished his walk of the perimeter of the room. "*And*, I'd like a private word with you to discuss *your note*."

CHAPTER THREE

LEO DISMISSED his men with a simple nod. They left promptly, Gilles leading the way to join the others outside.

The door closed quietly behind them.

After having completely resigned himself to never seeing her again, Leo marveled at the fact that he was mere feet from his one and only siren.

And he was itching to be alone with her.

Unable to stop himself, he devoured the vision she made. *Dieu*, she was so damned beautiful…

Even clothed in that plain dress and worn woolen shawl.

Her dark curly hair looked as silky as ever. He'd never forgotten the feel of those cool, luscious locks brushing against his skin. Or how soft they'd felt against his face as he buried it in the side of her neck and held her close.

And then there was that perfect mouth… He'd spent hours in oral worship of that mouth—and the rest of her edible little form. She hadn't graced him with one of her contagious smiles. He'd yet to see that little dimple that always appeared at the corner of her mouth whenever she grinned. Or laughed. *Christ*, how he missed that. He hadn't realized just how much until this very moment.

By God, he was going to coax a smile from her just so he could see her face light up once more.

Growing up, she'd always been exceptionally pretty, her

delightfully unorthodox ways adding to her charm. Yet, by the time she was a grown woman, she was so alluring she knocked him back on his heels. On sight.

Before, and now.

Every fiber of his being was rioting for her. His blood rushed through his body, white-hot. And his heart—that shriveled-up black thing—had swollen to life with emotion the moment he'd set eyes on her again.

His prick wasn't making the situation any easier. Not while the memory of those delicious moans and adorable little whimpers she'd made as he rode her to ecstasy and back flooded his mind.

And certainly not while she'd moved her gaze over his body in that tactile little perusal she had just given him.

He knew that look.

That look meant trouble.

For him.

Though he was immensely glad there was a level of interest on her part, something he would most definitely build on, this was a matter that required finesse and a slow, patient approach. When, at the moment, she was inspiring anything but patience in him.

He was so fucking hard, he wanted to howl.

Worse, the urge to march across the shop, tilt her head back with a tender tug of that beautiful hair, and claim her mouth was barely tamable—to hell with their little audience.

He'd had to purposely focus on the items in her shop, using the time and distraction to collect himself.

He'd spent the last seven years combing the realm, looking for another Suzanne Matchet.

There wasn't a single female who did what she did to him.

As usual, with no effort on her part whatsoever, she'd leveled him with the very same mind-bending desire and soft sentiments she alone incited.

Merde, if he had any good sense at all, he'd simply offer the apology he owed her for the hurt he'd caused her, turn, and leave—completely abandon this notion of revisiting the past. Any female who had this kind of impact on a man was far too dangerous to pursue.

But wild horses couldn't drag him from the room.

He'd combat the justifiable guardedness she felt—no matter how much it bothered him to see it. Especially when they'd once been so close. He'd eventually coax that stiffness from her delicate shoulders. He wasn't about to abandon her with Christmas approaching. Nor was he walking away from this miraculous opportunity to attend to something that had long been denied and left unfinished in his life.

You traveled all the way from Montbrison to see if you'd still feel that intense pull to her.

Well, he had his answer. It was definitely there.

Stronger than ever.

"Your Grace…" She lifted her chin a notch. "My note was rather plain. I don't see what there is to discuss."

He smiled at the mention of that rather colorful note. "That it was, *chère.*"

Her frown was immediate. *Merde.* She'd taken exception to his endearment. If he hadn't been so enthralled by her presence, he wouldn't have made the blunder. Endearments at this point sounded empty, especially when she considered him to be a scoundrel of the lowest order.

Since her, he'd kept his affairs brief, impersonal, and recreational over the years. He wanted something different with Suzanne. Something far more authentic. Raw. Real. He wanted her complete surrender. Heart. Body. And soul. He'd had enough empty encounters to last a lifetime.

He was going to have to be more careful with his word choices.

She gave a sharp sigh. Leo knew she was about to ask him to take his leave.

"Allow me a few minutes of your time," he said, stemming her words. He kept his tone calm and cajoling. "I've traveled a long way to speak to you. I would very much appreciate a private word."

"Come, Lucille. We should retire to the back room," said one of the older women.

He couldn't agree more. *Bloody hell, yes. Leave. Now!*

The scowl Lucille gave her companion said it all. Much to his frustration, he could see she harbored no desire to depart from the room.

Suzanne raised her hand, discouraging any retreat. "That isn't necessary, Rosalie." Then to him, she added, "We're quite busy, I'm afraid. We have a number of ointments and elixirs to prepare. I don't have time to spare."

He wasn't surprised by her answer. Nor was he deterred.

"Very well, then. I shall tell you what I came to say with our audience present. I came here for three reasons."

Four, actually—but he wasn't going to apologize for his transgressions in front of the two women in the room. It deserved a private moment.

"First, I came to offer you my sympathies in person. Regrettably, I've only recently learned of your father's passing." Though they meant well, it vexed him that his family hadn't mentioned something as monumental as Richard Matchet's death to him. The subject of Suzanne and her father was rarely—if ever—spoken about in front of Leo once they'd left Montbrison. A habit his siblings had formed on their own. "There are few men like your father. He graced this earth with his intellect and his gift of medicine. He left a lasting impression on all those fortunate enough to know him," he said about a man who deserved more than a handful of words.

That garnered soft sobs from both of the older women in the room. Stock-still, Suzanne merely listened with unshed tears glistening in her beautiful eyes.

Leo selected his next words with care, knowing they touched upon the delicate subject of their parting. "Though he left Montbrison, resigning his post, he never once abandoned my family. A few weeks later, on the night Aurore fell gravely ill, burning with fever, he didn't hesitate to rush to her aid and heal her." A slight smile lifted the corner of his mouth. "I still recall his arrival late at night, with a large pouch of his usual rose hips in hand."

She looked down for a moment and swallowed hard. When she finally met his gaze, she lifted a hand to her chest and absently rubbed it lightly over her heart. As though she were trying to soothe away an ache inside.

It broke his heart to see it.

He'd felt his own profound sorrow when he'd learned about her father's death. He could only imagine the grief she harbored at the loss of her beloved sire.

Merde. He wanted to cross the room so badly, draw her close, and comfort her. Always strong and brave, she didn't succumb to tears easily. In fact, he'd only ever seen it once, when they were young children and she'd fallen and horribly bloodied her knee racing with him and his brothers across the gardens at Montbrison. Even then, she'd held back the tears until his brothers were gone, shedding them before Leo alone. She'd trusted him.

Up until the day he destroyed her trust.

"Your father had and will always have the admiration and regard of my entire family. Myself included." It was something he wanted her to know, lest she had any doubts. Leo had held Richard Matchet in high esteem his entire life. He was a decent man to the core, unlike others Leo knew. The realm bowed to Leo's every whim, eager to align themselves with the riches, power, and influence of the d'Ermart family.

Yet he utterly despised it, hating all the social maneuvering and backstabbing at court and in the salons of Paris just to vie for his favor.

"Thank you…" she said softly. "Your kind words about my father are much appreciated. I trust you received our sympathies for your father's passing."

Leo's father had died months after Leo's marriage to Constance. He'd never had the enviable bond with his father that Suzanne had shared with Richard.

"I did. Thank you." He'd responded to Richard's letter of condolences with a note of thanks that, clearly, Richard had never shared with his daughter. As the loving parent Richard was, it appeared he'd only mentioned Leo to Suzanne when he absolutely had to, no doubt to spare her further upset.

"Good." She gave a nod. "You're welcome."

Dieu. She couldn't look more uncomfortable. He knew it would take time before she'd be relaxed in his presence and learn to trust him again, but her body was as rigid as the wooden shelves in her shop. *Dismiss our audience, beautiful Suzanne. Let me coax away that tension between us…*

There was a shadow of sadness in her eyes he knew had to do with her father's passing. Leo wanted to be the man in her life now. The one she turned to whenever she needed solace.

"I… Well… I really must return to my work now. Thank you again. If you'll excuse me…"

She was pulling further away. Not surprising in the least. Yet, the more she pulled away, the more determined he was to conquer the distance.

"You're most welcome, but I have more to say. The second reason I'm here is to convince you to come back with me to Montbrison. There is no reason for Richard Matchet's only daughter to be alone at Christmas, her charming note notwithstanding. Especially when she is so very welcome at the d'Ermart château."

Rosalie poked Lucille in the ribs. "Did you hear that, sister? *She's so very welcome.*"

"Shhh!" Lucille shot back. The woman was so singularly focused on their conversation, Leo was sure that the entire town could have burned down around her without her noticing.

"I would very much like to surprise Elisabeth and Aurore each with a gift of your wonderful perfume," he said truthfully. "I know they'd be delighted to receive it. They would be even more delighted by your company during the festive season. *As would I.*" He smiled.

"Really?" That charming little crinkle formed as she furrowed her brow. "I have a question for you, Your Grace."

"*Oh?* And what would that be?"

"Are you in possession of a single scruple?" She crossed her arms. "Perhaps you've forgotten that you have a *wife?* Have you no regard for her *at all?* You would have us both under the same roof after we had once—" She stopped abruptly. Then shot a glance at her assistants, another adorable blush coloring her cheeks.

Rosalie and Lucille were caught leaning sharply to the right, trying to get physically closer so as not to miss a single word without actually moving from their spot.

They immediately righted themselves.

Leo crossed his arms, mimicking Suzanne's pose. "That's three questions," he pointed out, still smiling.

Just being near her leavened his mood. Over time, he'd become humorless and brooding. And at the moment, he felt lighthearted for the first time in years.

"To answer your questions, I'm quite certain I possess some scruples." He thought for a moment and amended his statement. "Well, at the very least one or two." He lowered his arms and added more seriously, "And as for my wife, she is dead, Suzanne. It seems you are one of the few in the realm who has not heard of her demise."

Her eyes widened. "Oh... I-I... No. I didn't know. *I'm so sorry...*"

He sauntered toward her, keeping his approach to a slow, casual stride so that she wouldn't back away from him. He'd reached his limit. He couldn't stand being in the same room and remaining on the other side of it. He had to get closer.

Leo stopped an arm's length from her.

At this proximity, he could detect her favorite jasmine-scented soap, which she made and used. His cock twitched in response. That same scent on any other woman would have had little effect on him. But on *this* woman, emanating from *her* skin, it dazzled his senses.

"Thank you for your sympathies. But we were quite

estranged for years," he said. "The salacious details of her fatal carriage accident have had gossipmongers wagging their tongues for some time. I thought you'd heard."

"*Salacious details?*"

"Yes, Constance died while with her lover, the Marquis de Chermont. Apparently, they were in the throes of passion when it happened. When their bodies were recovered, both Constance and Chermont were in a state of undress. Of course, there's the very real possibility that Chermont was still inside Constance before they were thrown from the carriage."

A distinct "*Oh, my…*" came from the corner where the two older women stood.

As for Suzanne, her lips parted. A mixture of astonishment and disbelief was etched on her features.

This was the most he'd ever spoken about Constance, with anyone. But the woman before him wasn't just anyone.

She had once been his closest confidant.

And that was yet another thing he missed: having her to speak with candidly.

No one had ever dared mention his wife's extramarital activities to his face while she was alive, or since her death—any more than one would ever mention the king's brother's penchant for young men to His Majesty.

But that didn't stop Leo from learning of the gossip. It was Gilles's job to report who was talking about him or his family. Who had dubious motives against them. It was all part and parcel of his inauthentic world.

"I-I don't know what to say," she responded at last.

"You don't need to say anything—except that you will return with me to Montbrison."

"No, Your Grace. That is out of the question. I'm not free to leave, even if I wished it. With my father gone, there is no one else to tend to these good people's illnesses and injuries. I am needed here."

She was as brilliant a physician as her father had been, and everyone knew it—the Royal Academy of Sciences be damned.

He knew all too well how frustrated she felt in not being permitted admission simply because she was a woman. He'd not been able to change the mind of a single boorish fool in the Royal Academy. The king was just as narrow-minded.

Leo had always been proud of her abilities and her undaunted determination not to let her brilliant mind go to waste.

"Yes, I had thought of that," he said. "And I have a solution." He turned on his heel and stopped directly in front of the window of her shop. "Come take a look."

*****

SUZANNE WAS STILL reeling over his last revelation.

His wife's untimely end and the circumstances surrounding it were startling enough.

What on earth did he have waiting for her outside?

He leaned a shoulder against the window frame, stood there, all masculine magnificence, waiting patiently for her to join him, sporting that inviting smile she knew all too well—the very one that led women to their ruin.

Herself included.

She gazed back at him, unsure what to do. Then cast a glance at Rosalie and Lucille. They both nodded vigorously, wanting her to join Leo at the window.

Curiosity finally got the better of her.

All right. She'd take a peek.

Bracing herself for his next surprise, she crossed the room, then stopped by Leo's side and peered out the window.

"I believe you recognize Rolland Henry?" Leo said, looking quite proud of himself.

She couldn't believe her eyes.

Standing outside the carriage with Leo's men was indeed the tall, lanky man who had been her father's protégé. The breeze blew back Rolland's sand-colored hair. Both he and his brother Aron had been exceptional pupils and had worked closely under her father's tutelage for five years before becoming physicians in the town of Nort, an hour's ride away.

"He has agreed to stay here and attend to the ill in your absence," Leo said.

For the first time since she was a child, she had the urge to punch someone.

One particular d'Ermart.

Square on his aristocratic jaw.

"You have certainly gone to a lot of trouble." She returned Rolland's friendly smile and gave him a wave hello, despite the vexation that roiled through her.

Leo's smile now turned into a grin. "I'm glad you think so—"

"Oh, absolutely. You've completely won me over with this gesture alone."

"*Have I, now?*" There was a tinge of disbelief in his tone. He knew her well. He was unconvinced by her words.

"Definitely, Your Grace. What woman wouldn't be charmed by the notion that you dragged Rolland away from the sick just for your little Christmas seduction?"

She fumed.

The door on this part of her life had been closed. Never to be reopened again. And yet, it had been slammed wide open— unexpectedly—by a ghost from her past. A tall, dark, and presumptuous one.

"I shall spare you any more trouble. I am not interested in becoming your next tumble."

An easy smile formed on his handsome face once more. "This isn't simply about sex. And for your information, I made certain to provide Rolland's brother with a number of assistants so that he is well able to tend to those in need, before asking Rolland to come here."

"Then you admit that sex is part of your goal."

Leo glanced over her shoulder. Suzanne knew, without having to turn around, that Lucille and Rosalie were completely agog over this newest turn in the conversation.

And at the moment, she didn't care a whit.

She had bigger problems—and the biggest problem was standing right in front of her.

He dipped his head and lowered his voice. "Seven years ago, I lied to you. I made false promises just to have you. I said whatever I had to say in order to seduce you—that we'd be together always, when I knew full well that wasn't going to be the case. I won't lie to you again. I am not simply hunting for my next conquest. I've come here just for you. We had something incredible between us once. I think it is worth revisiting."

He was standing so close. She was too aware of the heat from his body for her liking. Worse, he had that sincere look in his eyes. The one that had deceived her years ago.

In retrospect, it was completely laughable that she'd once harbored the idea of being Leo's wife—a man who would one day become duc. But back then, she was so young, so utterly in love with him, she never doubted his assurances.

Clearly, her own foolishness was as much to blame for her heartache as his trickery.

After all the hurtful things he'd said upon their parting, she left Montbrison not just feeling deeply betrayed, but also angry at herself for her own idiocy.

He leaned in farther, bringing his mouth close to her ear. "I won't deny it. I want you. You are beautiful...desirable...so naturally sensual...and highly responsive..." Ever so lightly, he stroked the tip of his nose down her cheek. "And you smell so good..." The sensation sent a tiny quiver lancing into her belly.

The unwanted reaction irked her further still.

After all that had transpired between them, she shouldn't be responding to him.

He lifted his head, forcing her to look into his disarming eyes. They were a rare color she'd always marveled at. So similar to the rare jade miniatures prized by Leo's late father at Montbrison.

"There is much that has been left unfinished between us. Come with me to Montbrison," he gently urged. "It's home. To both of us. Come spend time with my family. With me." He dipped his head a mere fraction, his mouth hovering just above hers. "Let me show you how good—if not better—it can be now." His breath warmed her lips.

No. Not again. Suzanne immediately shored up her defenses, quashing the fluttering in her stomach.

She was stronger now. And far wiser. She wasn't going to succumb to the sensual timbre in his voice. Or the heated look in his pale green eyes. She had no reason to trust him. Or believe a thing he said.

She wasn't going to give him a second chance to play her for a fool.

Promptly, she stepped back, putting distance between them. This was just a game to him. He was nothing but a bored aristo merely seeking his latest distraction.

And he was going to have to seek his bed sport elsewhere.

"Though it would be delightful to see your sisters, I decline your offer to join you at Montbrison. *Again.* If your sisters wish me to create perfumes, they need only ask. I'd be delighted to oblige them."

He shook his head. "I won't leave you here alone at Christmas. Come now, Suzanne… Dismiss your servants. Let us talk about what happened between us seven years ago. In private."

"I'm very aware of what happened seven years ago. No discussion needed. I surrendered my innocence to a cad."

She heard more gasps come from behind her. Truthfully, this was the quietest Lucille or Rosalie had ever been in four years.

"True," he agreed. "A different man stands before you today."

"You mean to tell me you're not the rake everyone purports you to be? My word, Your Grace, what a grave injustice you've suffered to your reputation." Her sarcasm didn't perturb him in the least.

He looked more amused by her comment than annoyed.

In fact, he was actually *smiling.* *What is it going to take to send him away?*

"I've missed your fire, Suzanne. And I disagree. The grave

injustice occurred seven years ago when I let you go." He took a step toward her, bringing all that muscle and sinew closer again.

How she wished he'd stop doing that.

She rooted her feet to the floor, refusing to back away this time, determined to be impervious to his proximity. To him.

"I still remember the magic that we once made, the connection we once had. I still remember how good it feels to be around you…talking…laughing…*kissing…*" Leaning in, he whispered in her ear, "And I vividly remember how good it feels to be inside you."

On second thought, physical distance probably is best.

She moved over to the hearth and directed her gaze to a much more neutral sight—the mixture warming over the fire—and began to stir it.

She didn't want to spar with Leo. Especially when she was feeling so emotionally depleted from her father's death. The stubborn aristo was leaving. This minute. For her sanity's sake.

She acted on the first plan that entered her mind. Over her shoulder she tossed out, "Yes, well… Thank you for the visit. I must return to work. Please give my regards to your family. And you need not be concerned about my being lonely during the fête. I will be spending it with a very special male."

*****

A FEELING OF possessiveness slammed Leo in the gut.

Damn, Gilles. This was the sort of information he was supposed to provide. Gilles had told him there had been no one else in the last seven years.

The unwanted image of another man holding Suzanne, touching her, his mouth on her soft lips, burned through his brain. *Merde.* He'd no right to feel possessive of her. But that did nothing to quell the foreign emotion churning in his vitals.

He wasn't afraid of competition for her affections. That was hardly going to make him retreat, especially now that he'd seen her again—and those little compelling glimpses of her attraction to him when she'd let her guard slip.

He was going to woo his dark-haired beauty back into his arms. For good. But this tidbit of news had just made the situation of winning her back a greater challenge than he anticipated.

Glancing over at the two older women, he noticed the expressions on their faces. Their mouths were agape and their eyes were wide. Not that their looks had changed since his arrival. But it was their surprised reaction to Suzanne's romantic interest that gave him pause.

"We are quite taken with each other," Suzanne added as she gave whatever was boiling in the pot a stir.

"*Who is she talking about?*" Rosalie's loud whisper rose from their corner of the room.

It was Lucille's turn to poke Rosalie in the ribs. "*Hush!*"

According to Gilles, Lucille and Rosalie had been in Suzanne's employ for a few years. Given how keen they were about knowing the details of Suzanne's personal affairs—no matter how impertinent that was—how was it that they were unaware of this man?

Leo was beginning to have niggling doubts about the existence of his rival.

This wasn't simply a ploy to get rid of him, was it? She hadn't faced him when she spoke about her *very special male*. And she still had her back to Leo. He knew her as well as he knew himself. Was she afraid to turn around, knowing he'd be able to detect if she were lying if he saw her face?

He fought back a smile.

Oh, this was going to be fun. Matching wits and wiles with the spirited Suzanne Matchet had always been highly enjoyable.

"Is that so? Where did you meet him?" he asked, waiting for her response in order to gauge the reaction of the prying women in the room.

"He simply appeared at my door one day. He's very handsome, with attractive blue eyes." Her back was still to him.

Turn around, ma belle. Let me see those gorgeous readable eyes of yours.

"Hmm… Sounds rather mysterious. Does he have a name?"

She turned around and looked him square in the eye. "Gaspard," she said firmly, without a moment's hesitation.

Rosalie let out a squeak. Lucille slapped her hand over her sister's mouth.

The cat near the hearth gave a meow.

What the hell was he to make of *that*?

Suzanne had never been a good liar. Yet, she didn't fidget as usual. There were no actual signs of deception in her statement. Nor in how she delivered it. She continued to hold his gaze, ignoring the antics of the other two in the room.

Before he could delve further, someone entered the shop.

"Good day, Mademoiselle Matchet. I'm terribly sorry. I hope I am not interrupting. I saw the carriage outside and wasn't certain it was permissible to come in…" The woman who spoke was only slightly older than Suzanne. Beside her, a girl of about six held her hand. Their clothing, though not overly costly, did indicate they had some means. Perhaps the wife of one of the wealthier merchants in the town. "My lord." She gave him a deep curtsy. She, like Lucille and Rosalie, had had her eyes fastened to him from the moment she saw him.

"Good day, Madame Sebron," Suzanne responded with a welcoming smile. "It's quite all right. You are always welcome." She was nervous. More so, all of a sudden. He could tell, even if the others in the room seemed quite oblivious to it.

"We have a duc in our midst, madame!" Rosalie blurted out with great exuberance.

"Yes, thank you, Rosalie." Leo caught the slight tightness in Suzanne's tone. Why on earth was she so on edge at the arrival of this woman and child? "Your Grace, may I introduce you to Madame Sebron, and her daughter, Colette. Madame, the Duc de Mont-Marly."

"Oh, this is so very exciting! Your Grace, I am deeply honored to make your acquaintance." Madame Sebron gave him another curtsy. The child mimicked her mother.

Leo responded with a nod, then clasped his hands, mentally

cursing his ever-growing audience. Before he could utter any words, Suzanne interjected. "The duc is a very busy man, as you may well understand, madame."

"Oh yes. Of course…"

"He was just leaving to attend to his duchy and its official business."

"No, I was not," he countered, smiling. "I have yet to conclude my business here."

The child broke away from her mother and rushed to Suzanne, throwing her arms around her waist affectionately. "Hello, mademoiselle!"

"And a good day to you, Colette." Warmly, Suzanne brushed an errant blonde curl from the girl's face, revealing a pink, winter-chilled cheek.

"I asked Maman to bring me along to pick up Papa's stomach elixir," the child announced happily. "I like coming here. It smells good."

Suzanne laughed. "I'm glad you think so, my sweet. Lucille, would you please fetch Monsieur Sebron's stomach remedy from the back room."

Lucille left to do her bidding.

Suzanne waited for Lucille to return, her heart thundering so loud, she worried Leo would hear it.

She couldn't believe her bad luck! The arrival of Madame Sebron and Colette couldn't have been more ill timed. She'd told Leo an idiotic lie about Gaspard. Well, more a half-truth; sadly, her gray cat was indeed the only meaningful male in her life at the moment. But Leo didn't need to know that. The last thing she wanted was for Leo to discover her ruse. Especially when she saw how the news had unbalanced him—and hopefully dissuaded him.

The problem at hand was little Colette.

She liked Gaspard. Very much.

At any moment she could begin rooting around the room, looking for him, and give away Suzanne's deception.

Leo was no fool. He would immediately discern the

mortifying truth—that she'd meant the cat all along. Suzanne couldn't even move Gaspard to her private apartments upstairs—or do anything to bring attention to him—for that would surely prompt an immediate reaction from Colette.

Suzanne was now faced with the dilemma of rushing Madame Sebron and her daughter from her shop quickly, before either noticed her pet near the fire, all while not offending her faithful patients. Their patronage was something she just could not lose.

She prayed she could distract them until they left on their own accord. Once again she had that same strong urge overcome her. The one that made her want to punch Leo. She wouldn't be in this ridiculous predicament if it wasn't for him.

"Rosalie, why don't you show Colette our newest soaps? They smell so pretty, I just know she'd like to see them."

Rosalie wasted no time in complying and drew Colette to the corner of the room, far away from Gaspard.

Lucille was back in an instant, panting slightly from the exertion, and handed the vials to Madame Sebron. Suzanne knew Lucille had rushed out of fear—not just because she didn't want to miss a thing, though there was definitely that. But, judging from the agitated look in her eyes, she fully understood the urgency of the Sebrons' departure, and she was doing her best not to expose Suzanne's fabrication to Leo.

For that act of loyalty alone, Suzanne wanted to throw her arms around her.

Madame Sebron leisurely opened her coin purse, burrowed her gloved fingers inside, and began to root about for her money. The sheer slowness of her actions was maddening. Suzanne desperately hoped Gaspard was fast asleep behind her and wouldn't pick this moment to stretch his legs and parade about the room.

"Here you are." Madame Sebron held out her payment.

Finally...!

Lucille took the coins from her hand swiftly yet thankfully.

"Thank you, madame," Suzanne added. "Please let me know

if you need anything else. I'd be more than pleased to visit tomorrow to see how your husband is getting on, if you wish."

"Thank you. That would be very much appreciated." She returned Suzanne's smile. "Come, darling." Madame Sebron held out a hand to her daughter. "Let's return home to see how your father is feeling."

The child raced to her mother's side, clasped her hand, and bid everyone a cheerful *adieu*.

The door closed behind them.

Elation and relief rushed through Suzanne. *Thank God...* She gave Rosalie and Lucille a grateful smile.

The door crashed open.

Colette shot past, a gust of cold wind and her flouncing blonde curls trailing her. "I forgot to say good-bye to Gaspard!"

She dropped to her knees before him and gave him a loving stroke. "Good-bye, Gaspard. You're the most handsome cat I know. Stay warm." She petted his head, eliciting an appreciative purr, then shot back out the door, slamming it behind her.

The room froze.

As did Suzanne's breathing.

Her gaze darted to Lucille and Rosalie. While Rosalie was engrossed in the cracks on the ceiling, Lucille was looking down at the floor, utterly avoiding eye contact with Leo.

He's caught you in your lie. You're going to have to look at him sooner or later, Suzanne. What were the chances that the floor would open and swallow her up? Or him?

Reluctantly, she dragged her gaze over to Leo.

His arms were crossed, and he was grinning from ear to ear. He lowered himself down onto his haunches, and beckoned Gaspard to him. A normally willful cat, Gaspard didn't hesitate to stroll across the floor and obey.

Leo scooped him up, then rose, lightly scratching Gaspard under his chin, a litany of contented purrs emanating from her pet.

Traitor.

"I must agree," Leo said, still grinning. "Gaspard is definitely handsome with attractive blue eyes."

Mentally she cringed and was back to blushing, beyond embarrassed. Her lie was so pathetic. Could she make it any more plain how bare her life had become?

Leo sauntered over to her and placed the cat in her arms. "But I can do much more for you than Gaspard ever could."

"There we agree, Your Grace. He's never wreaked the havoc in my life that you have," she pointed out.

His smile faded. "You never deserved the pain I inflicted on you. Allow me the chance to make amends."

"There is no need. I no longer think of you as my closest friend. Or the love of my heart."

His voice dropped to the softest, most knee-weakening pitch as he said, "I still do."

That knocked her off guard.

She quickly shook off the effect of that measured sentence, reminding herself that he knew just what to say, how to say it, and what to do to impact a woman's senses. He was a master of seduction.

"Your Grace, you are quite adept at applying your charm. But I've heard soft words from you before. And I am no longer gullible. I have no faith in your romantic utterances."

There was a ghost of a smile on his mouth. "That's understandable. I'll have to prove to you the depths of my sincerity. I'm going to show you just how contrite I am. I won't leave Maillard without you. Make no mistake. I'll be waiting for you outside until you decide to return to Montbrison with me."

She laughed. "Surely you aren't serious, Your Grace. You risk freezing off a part of your male anatomy you're rather fond of." She immediately regretted her word choices the instant she saw him cock a brow in amusement.

He leaned in, his dark hair lightly brushing her cheek. The tiny sensation rippled through her body. "I can't tell you how delighted I am by your interest in my cock," he said in her ear. She could hear the smile in his voice. "Since you brought up the subject, the part you refer to is at the moment eager and hard, just being near you again."

He pulled back, still smiling.

Thanks to his cheeky comment, the urge to peek at the bulge in his breeches was suddenly overwhelming.

Good God, don't look…

"It's a relief to know you haven't become burdened with any sort of modesty," she said, trying to eradicate thoughts of his generous sex from her mind.

He chuckled and shrugged. "You were the one who mentioned it. I was only trying to alleviate your concern."

Suzanne managed to keep her gaze fixed to his face, even while the unwanted memory of how incredible it felt to have his large, solid length inside her flooded her head. That delicious stretching sensation of her private muscles as he fed her every delectable inch of his cock was a memory she had long suppressed. Until now. He'd driven her wild. Not just because of his sexual expertise—though he was undoubtedly gifted in the carnal arts. But because she'd shared the experience with *him*.

It was *his* mouth on hers.

His hands on her body.

Her Leo—or at least that was what she'd believed then.

She reasserted herself. "I do believe you've taken this attempt at a tumble far enough. The past is best left in the past. We have both moved on, in opposite directions—in keeping with our different social standing. There are other women in your class you can chase. Please seek your amorous encounters there."

He glanced past her shoulder. "I think you've seen and heard enough," he said to Lucille and Rosalie. "Please give us a private moment."

Before Suzanne could say a word, Lucille snatched Gaspard from her arms and rushed out the door with her sister, retreating to the back room. Leaving Suzanne stunned.

And alone with Leo.

Clearly, loyalty was short-lived around here.

She turned to face him. Leo caught her cheeks between his palms and swooped in for a kiss, possessing her mouth on a gasp. Her sex clenched fiercely at the first stroke of his tongue. A jolt of heat rocked her so hard, she felt it reverberate all the way down to her toes.

She jumped back, alarmed, breaking contact. Her breathing shallow and sharp. Her insides quivered in the aftermath. Worst of all, there was the lightest, most persistent ache pulsing in that bud between her legs.

"*Dieu.* I knew it was still there," he murmured with a smile. He slipped his fingers under her chin and tilted her head back, his mouth so close to her sensitized lips. Her breath froze in her throat. She was unsure if he was going to kiss her again. Unsure how she felt about another kiss while her long-dormant nerve endings hummed with life. "We had something very rare once. It would be a horrible shame not to see if we can recapture it. It isn't the sort of connection that happens every day." He brushed his lips against hers, a tantalizing feather-like stroke. "I'll be waiting for you outside."

He released her and walked to the door.

She immediately dismissed the flicker of disappointment that whispered through her. Placing his hand on the door handle, he turned to face her. "Oh, and you're not getting another kiss until we get to Montbrison."

He gave her a wink and left.

CHAPTER FOUR

"HE IS STILL out there. It's been *two days*!" Rosalie craned her neck as she and her sister peered out the window for what was likely the thousandth time since Leo had set up camp outside. A warm fire blazed right in the middle of the road, forcing everyone to reroute around him, as His Highness casually reclined in a settee—a mere portion of the furniture that had been brought out for his comfort from the inn across the street.

"The weather could easily turn. He's going to catch his death," Lucille added, fretful.

Not if Suzanne killed him first.

As luck would have it, the weather was working against her. What little dusting of snow they'd had this unseasonably warm winter was completely gone. The last two days and nights had been the mildest she'd seen in weeks. Leo was bearing the warmer temperatures easily—without any distress at all. She, on the other hand, hadn't slept since his arrival. If she wasn't thinking about Leo's inflaming kiss, she was plagued with concerns over this ludicrous situation he'd created.

And the stir he'd made in the town.

Was he ever going to leave? Surely, he was getting tired of being out there.

No?

As Leo's men and the innkeeper catered to him throughout the day, making certain that he had a constant supply of food and drink, people from all over Maillard were descending on her shop just to catch a glimpse of one of the most powerful ducs in the realm. Most had never been in the proximity of a man from such elevated bloodlines. Yet, Leo seemed totally oblivious to the crowds as he sat comfortably reclined—hands laced behind his head and legs crossed at the ankles—with his attention fixed on her shop. And a contented smile on his face. It appeared he had no idea that he was causing townspeople to flock to her shop, interrupt her work, just to inquire why the duc was stationed outside her door.

She was tempted to tell them she was treating him for excessive flatulence.

Instead, she politely suggested they direct their questions to the Duc de Mont-Marly himself—knowing none would ever be so bold.

Suzanne pulled a hard wooden bowl off the shelf, threw in a handful of almonds, and started on Madame Rideau's indigestion remedy. Trying—needing—to keep busy. Using her pestle, she pulverized the almonds with great zeal, venting some frustration.

"Oh, you simply must see what the duc is wearing today, Suzanne," Rosalie said, all aflutter over this whole ordeal. "He is looking so very handsome. Princely, I'd say. I've never seen such costly material!"

Oh no. Absolutely not.

Suzanne wasn't about to go anywhere near that front window. Leo had made it a habit to remain outside until well past midnight each night before retiring to his room at the inn.

The man had caught her peeking at him from her second-floor bedroom window directly above her shop. Every time.

Each time, he'd grin and wave.

Or blow her a discreet kiss.

He was driving her to distraction.

"I'm certain his attire is wonderful," she said, smashing more almonds. "Rosalie, would you please fetch me the mustard seeds? Lucille, kindly check on the roasting oats for Monsieur

Marchey's purgative." Hopefully that would draw the two women away from the window. Leo didn't need more people gawking at him.

And she did not need any more recounts of how attractive he was.

"I have the mustard seeds right here." Rolland sported his usual cheery smile and held up the clay jar he'd just obtained from the back room. "And I've just checked on the roasting oats. They look almost ready."

She stopped pulverizing the almonds, took a deep breath, and schooled her features, knowing she was scowling. Neither Rolland nor her assistants should be at the receiving end of one of her scowls.

That should be reserved strictly for the exasperating, single-minded duc living outside her door.

"Thank you, Rolland. You've been an incredible help these past two days. It has been very much appreciated." Having Rolland around again was both wonderful and painful. It brought back bittersweet memories of her father and his years of working with the young doctor. It only made her miss her sire more.

And that, too, she blamed on Leo.

If that weren't enough, there was an entirely different issue currently eroding what little mental peace she had left. One that had invaded her thoughts in the wee hours of the morning.

What in the world was the third reason?

Leo had told her he'd come for three reasons. The first was to offer his condolences. The second was to convince her to return with him to Montbrison.

But, after a second night void of any repose, as she lay in bed staring at the ceiling, it occurred to her he'd never told her the third.

Why are you wasting a moment's thought on any of this? In her mind's eye, she could still see Leo's impassive face as he told her that their night together had meant nothing to him and that he was marrying another.

She had been doing her best to get on with her life—without her father—before Leo's arrival. Leo was only making things more challenging for her. Her father's death had been so sudden and unexpected. Leaving a gaping void in her life. And now that he was gone, she fought to live in the moment and not drown in sorrow. Or self-pity. Each morning she donned a mask of bravery and refused to anguish over the fact that she was alone.

Leo was a formidable force to contend with. He could cause far too much damage to a woman's heart if he was entrusted with it. He wasn't going to sweep in and level her world again when she was already struggling to keep it from collapsing. All she had to do was stay strong and not give in to Leo's seductive charms.

She'd wait it out. Leo couldn't remain outside indefinitely.

Then she could return to her life, or what was left of it.

She tossed more almonds into her bowl and crushed them, with little success in alleviating her distress.

Finally, she dropped her pestle in the wooden bowl. "I'll finish madame's elixir later. I'm going to the market."

Some fresh air and spending time demonstrating and selling her new matchsticks would do her good.

*****

LEO SAW SUZANNE exit her shop, basket in hand. He was on his feet in an instant.

Thank God… He was starting to go fucking mad with restlessness.

He'd never waited for any woman the way he'd waited for her. Further proof of how far gone he was when it came to this one particular female. He'd never put in this much effort for a woman. He never had to.

Suzanne was the only exception he'd ever made.

He hadn't followed her yesterday or the day before as she delivered her remedies and visited her patients. He'd given her some distance yet kept his presence known before her shop. But today, *Dieu*, today he was going to do something—*anything*—

that would move matters along and speed up her decision to come with him.

Before the weather changed and he bloody well froze his sac off.

He wasn't about to spend the entire winter living outside her shop—any more than he was going to give up and walk away without gaining a second chance.

An unexpected gust of wind blew the hood off her brown cloak. Gorgeous long dark curls rustled on the breeze and brushed away from the sweetest face he'd ever known.

His body ignited. *Jésus-Christ,* she made him ache. He was in love with her still. And there wasn't a damned thing he could do about it to make peace with it.

Except win her back.

She was part of the common class. Of ordinary origin. Yet, it was vastly apparent that even after being separated for years, he'd never recovered from the impact she'd made on him. He couldn't even tell her how he felt. At least not yet.

Voicing soft sentiment wasn't typical for him. She'd been the only one he'd ever uttered the words to. And given her reaction to his endearment the other day, at the moment, she'd only deem any of his amorous declarations to be false.

Suzanne cast him a glance, shook her head in dismay, then turned and walked off, her long cloak snapping sharply behind her.

Looking far too saucy.

His hungry prick pressed hard against the inside of his breeches.

Leo couldn't help but smile, despite the discomfort he was in. Only she could make saucy look tantalizing. Oh, the things he was going to do to her sweet little form when she was his again… He was going to put all that fire inside her to such delicious use.

He raced up and fell in step beside her. "Good morning, Suzanne."

She stared straight ahead, maintaining her rapid steps. "Please go away." She rubbed her cloak near her shoulder.

He took a brief moment to delight in the scent of jasmine emanating from her skin, and in the lines of her lovely profile. He'd always adored that endearing little nose.

"I'd be delighted to leave Maillard. When shall we depart?"

That arrested her steps. She turned and faced him squarely, her big brown eyes meeting his gaze firmly. "Your Grace, *we* are not departing. But I do hope you are."

"When are you going to start calling me Leo again?"

"At the moment, there are a number of names I'd like to call you. Leo isn't one of them," she said and resumed her strides, walking away from him.

He laughed. "Come with me to Montbrison, and you can tell me your favorites along the way," he called out, then caught up to her again. "You've got your matchsticks, I see. I saw your demonstration yesterday to one of your patients outside your shop. Very impressive," he said sincerely.

"Thank you." She reached up and rubbed her shoulder again.

"Is there something the matter with your shoulder?"

"No."

"Then why do you keep rubbing it?"

She stopped, and let out a sharp sigh before turning to face him again. "Because this is my lucky cloak. Good things happen to me when I rub it. Such as coming up with the much-needed solution of how to get the matchsticks to ignite by using a flour paste. But the cloak isn't working anymore."

He battled back a smile. She was still assigning good fortune to inanimate objects. "It isn't?"

"No. You are still here." Her voice was tinged with fatigue. He wondered if she was getting any more sleep than he was. Thoughts of her, of how near she was, had kept him up most of the night. "When are you going to give up this game?"

"I should think my waiting for you for the last two days would prove that this isn't a game. I am quite serious," he said. "And I'm not giving up."

"This is indeed a game. We've played many games as

children, and you have never liked to lose. You came here thinking you could use your polished manner and good looks, and I would give myself to you, as I did before. Yet, now you find yourself too entrenched in your charade, not willing to lose face—or retreat—and *that* is why you are still waiting outside. The more difficult the catch, the sweeter the prize, *no?* At least admit the truth."

It was true. He did hate to lose. And he'd lived with the staggering loss of her for too long. He wished he could tell her so and actually have her believe him.

Leo rested his hands on his hips to keep from reaching out and touching her. She was so skittish, he had no doubt she'd bolt if he tried.

A single silky curl tickled her cheek in the breeze. How he wanted to gently brush it behind her ear and pull her against him—more than he wanted his next breath.

"All right. Here are some plain truths. If all I wanted was sex, Suzanne, there's no need to sit outside your shop to wait for it. Or to come here at all. There has never been a short supply of willing women at court." He wasn't going to even remotely pretend he'd led the life of a celibate monk. As Constance basked in the glow of her affair, he'd delved into drink and debauchery.

Extensively.

"I would not be out here and risk freezing that part of my 'male anatomy I'm rather fond of,'" he said, repeating her earlier words, "if this was nothing more than bed sport. As for worrying about losing face, I'm no longer a child, playing childish games. With a childish mind. If I didn't give a damn what anyone thought when I'd been cuckolded by my wife, why would I suddenly be concerned about *'losing face'?* And since we are finally talking, here are some more truths: I had a duty to my family I could not shirk seven years ago. The marriage contract had been signed by both families weeks prior to our night together. And I knew it. I was well aware that as heir, I was going to have to marry a woman I barely remembered meeting, for the sake of the d'Ermarts' political gain and advancement of power," he said, practically sneering.

His familial obligations soured his insides and left a bitter taste in his mouth. He'd grown to despise his birthright long ago. His "privileged" birth had come at a vast personal cost. He'd been told throughout his life that as a d'Ermart, he could have anything he wanted.

A bloody lie.

What he'd wanted all along was the woman before him with the smudged shoes. And lucky cloak. "And yes, I purposely withheld the betrothal from you. I fought within myself, vacillating between staying away from you. Or acting on the carnal cravings we both harbored for each other. Finally, I chose the latter—when I had no right to—for one simple reason."

"*Oh?* And what was that?"

"I simply couldn't live a lifetime never knowing what it was like to make love to you."

That took her by surprise.

Her eyes widened, and he could have sworn there was a slight softening before she rapidly retreated back behind her defenses. *Merde.* Witnessing her apprehension to trust him yet again staggered him. This wasn't getting any easier to see. Not when they'd had the tightest bond once. Not when he'd been so accustomed to a very different Suzanne.

One who had the world of faith in him.

And he had no one to blame for her mistrust but himself and the horrible way he'd handled everything years ago.

"I miss the Suzanne who took chances and risks and did everything with great passion and zeal. Fearlessly. Take a chance today. Come home with me. Let us see what might be between us again. I was once the only person you allowed yourself to be truly open and vulnerable with," he reminded her softly. "Will you let me past the pain I caused? Lower those tall walls you have insulated yourself behind. Let me see that woman again. I know she is in there, waiting to be cherished. Allow me to be the one to cherish her. I know there is pain deep inside her. And grief. Let me help heal it. There is no one who knows her heart, body, and mind better than I do."

Briefly, Leo pressed a gentle finger over her heart. "Let me see inside here again," he whispered.

She looked away, then raised a hand and lightly tugged at her earlobe. There it was. That adorable odd little habit she had when she was deep in thought. His heart pounded away the moments. The mere fact that she was even contemplating his words was monumental.

When she met his gaze again, her beautiful brown almond-shaped eyes shone with heart-sinking distrust. She shook her head. "I have already lost one home because of you. I'm here to sell my matchsticks to ensure I won't lose another after you leave."

"I'm not going to leave."

"That's what you said the last time. Quite convincingly, I might add, just before I gave myself to you. And as I recall, shortly afterward you also said I was a good tumble, and that I was never meant to be more."

Fuck.

"I meant none of the things I said to you the day we parted. I admit I was a colossal ass. I thought if I made you hate me, it would make our parting easier for you. It would spare you pain afterwards."

"Well, it seems you failed on both counts. I didn't feel hate. And I did feel pain. At least we agree on the ass part."

She turned on her heel to leave. Leo caught her hand and, in one fluid motion, yanked her into a nearby alley, away from prying eyes, and pressed her back against the wall.

She gasped.

"What… What are you doing?" She couldn't have sounded more surprised. There was a slight panic in her voice.

He braced his palms against the wall on either side of her shoulders. "Since you won't allow me a moment alone with you, I'm seizing one."

Her gaze shot out to the street. "What if someone sees us?

What are they going to say? You've made enough of a spectacle—"

"They're not going to say a damned thing. I've ordered Gilles to make it clear to all the curious onlookers that the House of d'Ermart holds you and your father in the highest esteem and that we would consider it a gross personal insult for anyone to conduct themselves to the contrary toward you."

She squirmed anxiously. "Why are we here? You aren't going to kiss me, are you? You…you said you wouldn't kiss me again unless we were at Montbrison. Lying again, were you?"

Her nervous excitement was palpable.

So was that delicious fire that was smoldering between them. She wasn't fooling him. He knew that there was at least a part of her that wanted to be kissed, and it was unsettling her. His dark-haired beauty was using the taunt as a way to stave off the carnal intensity they both knew would spike on intimate contact.

"I promised I'd be honest with you. No lies," he assured her, though at the moment he wished he hadn't made the pledge not to kiss her unless at Montbrison. "Here is another truth. I know I hurt you deeply. It grieves me, more than you could ever know. And I am truly sorry for the pain I've caused." Leo slipped his fingers under her chin, bringing her mouth a fraction closer. *Jésus-Christ*, he wanted to slowly savor those luscious lips. "But I can't say that I'm sorry for our night together. That would be a lie. I count our night as one of the most incredible nights of my life."

Suzanne's heart raced.

She was in trouble.

Very big trouble.

His words were starting to have an effect on her. His apology had been completely unexpected, and it inspired a familiar emotional stirring. One that terrified her to the marrow.

If that weren't bad enough, the heat from his fingers was seeping through her system and pooling in her belly. She had the maddening urge to grab his ears and yank him to her. Anything that would give her a taste of his tempting mouth. And garner her physical contact with his hard-muscled form.

So, you crave to feel some real bliss…like the decadent pleasures Leo introduced you to.

But she wanted more than that. Beyond the physical. She wanted *love*. Real, unconditional love from a man whose affections would not be capricious. A love that was deep, unwavering, steadfast. A husband whose arms would comfort and strengthen her. A connection with honesty and respect that couldn't be broken. No matter what.

Just as her father had described he'd had with her mother.

You can't weaken now. This man is high nobility. A celebrated libertine with a trail of broken hearts left in his wake wherever he goes. And you are far beneath his station of birth.

Nothing good could come of this for you…

"As for the kissing, you do need to be kissed, Suzanne. Long and hard," he continued, his thumb lightly grazing her bottom lip with titillating effect. Her nipples tightened. "And at Montbrison, I intend to kiss you from your pretty mouth…all the way down to that delectable little bud between your legs." At the mention of that part of her anatomy, a hot pulse quivered through her core. Her knees almost buckled.

"But not until you beg for it," he whispered with a smile. Releasing her face, he pressed his hands against the stone wall again and tilted his head, keeping his mouth tantalizingly close. No doubt to escalate her hunger.

And, damn it, it was thoroughly working on her starved senses.

"Do you remember it, Suzanne? Do you remember how much you loved having your pretty pink clit in my mouth? I know how to build the pleasure…until you couldn't take it anymore. I know how to make you come so very hard…" Dear God. The ache between her legs that was growing fiercer with every soft, seductive word he spoke.

"We were once compatible in every way. Do you ever allow yourself to remember how good it was between us?" he asked. "Do you recall all the laughter and confidences we shared? The affinity was as potent as the carnal connection we had. Do you remember it?"

"I've done everything in my power to forget it. All of it," she said, hoping she sounded firm despite the chaos inside her.

She had to put an end to this, for the sake of her sanity. He was eliciting physical and emotional responses she wanted to quell.

Shoving a hand against his chest, she managed to move him back a bit. Ignoring the heat of his body against her palm. "What about you, Your Grace?" she countered, intent on turning the tables on him and hopefully quashing this conversation completely. "Since you've declared yourself to be an 'honest man' now, just how many times have you remembered any of it? How many times have I entered your thoughts in the past seven years?"

"You want the absolute truth?"

"Yes, the absolute truth." She found herself suddenly braced for his response, and she had no idea why.

"Once," he said.

"Oh."

Disappointment lanced through her. And she mentally chastised herself for it. It shouldn't matter what his response was.

He cupped her cheek with one hand. "You entered my thoughts only once, immediately after your departure from Montbrison, and you haven't left my mind since."

That sent a wild flutter in her stomach. "Oh…"

Will you stop saying, "Oh." Not exactly your most brilliant response. Dare you believe him?

He'd been back in her life for only a few days and he was already overwhelming her mind and body. She had to get away. She needed time to think. To catch her breath. And collect herself.

"I have to go," she said, hoping her voice sounded firm. Yet, her feet seemed stuck.

"Would you like to know what else I'm thinking?" His thumb

stroked her cheek, the sensation streaking down to the tips of her breasts. She couldn't suppress her shiver.

She pushed his hand away from her face, having difficulty concentrating when he touched her like that. "I'm certain it is scandalous in nature."

He chuckled. "Besides that. I'm thinking that part of you wants to come with me to Montbrison."

"No, I do not." She felt the immediate twinge, her heart objecting to her words. Late last night, she'd pictured herself back in Montbrison, a place that had been the happiest home she'd ever known. In her mind's eye, it was a beautiful Christmas, just as they used to be, surrounded by people who'd cared about her, like dear Elisabeth and Aurore.

But then there was Leo.

He was the obstacle.

She was too unsure what to make of him. And his words. Any of this.

A big purely male grin formed on his far too handsome face. "I think you do. You just need a little encouragement."

With that, he turned and walked away, disappearing around the corner.

What in the world is that supposed to mean?

CHAPTER FIVE

CRACKING OPEN AN eye, Suzanne immediately realized she'd overslept.

Something she'd never done before. The sun was bright and blazing through her window.

Another warm day, no doubt.

Another night with little more than two hours of sleep.

After the evocative encounter with Leo yesterday, she'd tossed and turned, pondering his words. And becoming frustrated with herself for neglecting to ask what his mysterious third reason was for coming to see her.

It was still ridiculously niggling at her. Adding to the ever-growing list of Leo-related torments that kept her up.

And then there's that apology…

What little repose she'd had was plagued with dreams of Leo. Hot carnal dreams where she'd given him carte blanche with her body.

Just as she had that night long ago.

And oh, how he'd utilized his natural carnal talents to bestow the most mind-melting pleasure.

Those vivid images filled Suzanne's mind, instantly heating her blood.

She rolled onto her side and squeezed her knees together, trying to combat the scintillating throbs coming from the bud between her legs. She was hungry for the one man who knew how to feed her famished senses.

The very man she could never have and hold forever.

Lucille's and Rosalie's elevated voices pierced the quiet, wafting up from her shop to her second-floor bedroom. It was their commotion that had awoken her in the first place.

And, God only knew the reason, it was only escalating.

They were being far too loud for her frayed nerves.

Suzanne groaned and pulled the covers over her head, trying to drown out the noise, wanting the world outside her room to go away. Yesterday had been a dismal failure. Neither the lace merchant nor the blacksmith's wife had had any money to pay her for their tonics, bringing the number of patients who now owed her payment to an unprecedented *seven*. And after three hours of trying, she'd sold the total sum of two matchsticks.

Clearly, her lucky cloak was dead.

All its wonderful luck had drained out.

The day Leo arrived.

What were the chances that he'd left for his grand château and this ordeal was over?

The door slammed open, startling her. Gaspard, sleeping on the corner of her bed, leapt to the ground with a sharp meow.

Rosalie was flushed and wringing her hands. "You've got to come. Right now."

Suzanne sat up, pulling the covers to her chest. "What's happened?"

"The entire town is here, and they are demanding to speak to you."

"The *entire* town?" she repeated, skeptical. Rosalie was known to exaggerate from time to time.

"Yes! THE ENTIRE TOWN! For God's sake, HURRY!"

*****

SUZANNE WASHED AND dressed in wild haste and flew down the stairs, clutching her shawl. She stopped dead in her tracks at the doorway.

Stunned by the sight before her.

A throng had descended upon her shop. Dear God, it truly did look as though the entire population of the town was there.

Lucille, Rosalie, Rolland, and two of Leo's men had managed to maneuver the crowd into some semblance of a line. A line that went well out the door of her shop, spilling onto the streets.

The moment they saw her, the mass surged toward her, a roar erupting.

She jumped back in surprise.

She caught a word here. And one there. But could make no sense of anything they were shouting.

"What is happening here?" Her voice barely carried over the chaos.

"The Duc de Mont-Marly," was all Lucille shouted in response as she and Rolland were trying to keep the three feisty Alard spinsters back, their red hair a perfect match for their temperament. The three stout middle-aged sisters couldn't have appeared more determined to get past them.

"He's commenced a contest," Rolland added, then to the three siblings at the front of the line, "Ladies, please. A bit of patience. You'll each have a turn."

A turn for what? "What sort of contest?" Suzanne barely finished her question when Camille Alard, the eldest not to mention the shortest of the Alard sisters, kicked Rolland in the shin. He yelped as she raced around him and grabbed Suzanne's hands.

"You should go with the duc to Montbrison because he is very handsome, and he has good teeth. You can always trust a man with good teeth."

Suzanne blinked. "*Pardon?*"

"Have I convinced you?" Camille asked, her hazel eyes wide, looking ever so hopeful.

Oh no. He couldn't have. He didn't... He wouldn't enlist the town to— "What in the world are you talking about?" Suzanne posed the question, praying she was wrong in her deduction.

"The Duc de Mont-Marly has offered ten *louis d'or* to the individual who convinces you to accompany him to his château and spend the upcoming fête with his family," Camille explained. "I think you are mad not to go."

Dear God, he did! And he's offering ten gold coins!

Suzanne's gaze shot up, taking in the mayhem once more. Normally placid townspeople were clamoring for her, pushing and shoving, trying to get closer. Those who were still outside, trying to get in.

"*Well?*" Camille prompted, impatient for her reply.

"I'm afraid not." Oh, she was going to kill Leo…

"Step aside." Marie Alard pushed her older sister out of the way, ignoring the protest she received from her sibling. "You should go with the duc and visit his family because you will have a lovely time with them. He has kind kin."

"How on earth would you even know that?" Suzanne asked, feeling frustrated and furious at the bane of her existence: Leo d'Ermart.

"Well, he looks as though he has kind kin," Marie reasoned. "Also, he told us so."

She couldn't believe Leo had done this.

She had to get out. There was a duc she needed to see. One she might push off the nearest cliff just so she could have some normalcy in her life again!

And perhaps some sleep.

Suzanne stepped around Marie but didn't get far. The youngest Alard sister immediately blocked her path.

"You should go with the duc to his château because he has wonderful shoulders. It's always much more pleasant to dine with a man with wonderful shoulders."

"I don't think so." Suzanne managed to get only another two feet when the shoemakers, Monsieur and Madame Falque, stepped in her way.

"The duc is delightful company," the wife said. The husband added, "He has excellent footwear!"

Actually, the duc makes me pant shamelessly, and I couldn't care less about what he sticks on his feet…

"If you'll please excuse me…" She inched her way out, all

while Leo's praises were bellowed at her from every direction. "He is very handsome!" "He is rich!" "He's utterly charming." "No one turns down a duc!"

"He lives in a grand palace!"

At last she breached the doorway.

Rising up onto the balls of her feet, she tried peering over the crowd, looking for Leo's camp.

It was gone.

In its place was a larger horde of townspeople than in her shop.

She took a deep breath and let it out slowly, then made her way across the street to the inn with as much dignity as one could muster while being jostled and verbally accosted with the attributes of the Duc of Mont-Marly.

It took many aloud *"Excuse me"* and *"Pardon me"* over the calamity, and several idiotic responses like, *"No, I don't think the duc's exceptional clothing and intellect are deciding factors,"* before she finally reached the inn.

After snatching open the door, Suzanne slammed it shut behind her, and locked it. She slumped against it, the roar of the crowd barely muffled by the barrier.

The innkeeper, Joseph, rushed to her. The tall, elderly gentleman was her father's age.

"Good day, Mademoiselle Matchet."

She was already marching across the room toward the stairs. "Good day, Joseph." She tried not to sound gruff toward the kindly man. "Which room is the Duc de Mont-Marly in, please?"

"He's on the second floor, mademoiselle. In the largest room we have—at the far end of the hall." Joseph cleared his throat. "And might I add…you should join the duc for the upcoming fête because he is, well, a duc, after all."

Et tu, Brute? Why was she suddenly feeling like Caesar in the book she'd read once from the d'Ermart library by the Englishman William Shakespeare? Leo had gotten to dear Joseph, too. "Thank you, Joseph. And I'm quite aware of his title."

"Well, perhaps you should consider that he is a wealthy man."

"I'm aware of that."

"With much power and influence."

"I'm aware of that, too."

"What about his enormous manhood?"

That stopped her dead in her tracks. She turned. "*Pardon?*"

Joseph turned dark crimson. "Oh, no…no, I…I didn't mean… What… What I meant to say is that he has great presence. He… He's a tall, masculine man. The very kind women like. A very manly man…Not… Not to suggest that you have any interest in the duc in that regard! Or… Or to imply there is anything untoward about his invitation…I'm… I'm needed in the kitchen. Please, excuse me…" He rushed off, rubbing the back of his neck.

She shook her head.

Fuming, Suzanne raced up to Leo's room. She raised her fist and pounded on the door.

The door was snatched open.

Standing there was the one and only Leo d'Ermart.

His dark hair wet. Wearing nothing but his black breeches. Her heart missed a beat. She watched as two water droplets dripped from his hair onto his shoulder. And ran down his skin.

One along his chest.

And the other down the length of one muscled arm.

It was the most riveting sight she'd ever seen.

Her cheeks grew hot. Her whole body warmed. That familiar hunger roared through her senses. She couldn't tear her gaze away, devouring every devastating inch of him. Seized by the urge to run her hands over every dip and ripple on his chiseled chest and sculpted abdomen.

Upon seeing her, a slow smile formed on his lips. He raked a hand through his hair. "Good day, Suzanne."

Her mouth felt dry. Her nipples were tight, pressing against the inside of her chemise.

Dear God… Focus!

"What…" Her voice came out as a mortifying squeak. She swallowed hard and tried again, with a more forceful tone this time. "What do you think you're doing?" she demanded.

He leaned his forearm against the doorframe. She tried ignoring the appealing flex of his bicep that came naturally with the movement. "I just finished my bath. What a shame. You could have joined me."

Her sex moistened at the mere suggestion.

Standing this close to him, seeing that wicked gleam in his light green eyes, and with nothing more than the simple cloth of his breeches covering his muscled form, it was very difficult to give him a piece of her mind.

Not when her mind was on his skin—remembering how warm and delicious it was. His strong arms, and the incredible feel of being in their embrace.

And then there was that generous, utterly noticeable bulge in his breeches. Knowing he wanted her made her clitoris pulse in time with her quickened heart.

How was it possible that he drew her just as powerfully as he had all those years ago when he'd melted her heart?

"I have a question," she said, pushing away the past.

"Ask whatever you like. I'll be truthful."

"That's excellent. What I want to know is—are you deranged?"

"I don't believe so."

"Do you know I cannot leave my shop? I cannot even BE IN my shop, for I am assailed with people trying to convince me to come with you to Montbrison—just to win the fortune you have dangled before them!"

Amused, he cocked a brow. "Have any succeeded?"

"Only in inspiring thoughts of your demise."

He chuckled, reached out, and captured her hand. "Don't just stand there. You can tell me all the things you want to do to my body inside." With that, he yanked her into the room and shut the door.

She was suddenly alone with the all too alluring Duc de

Mont-Marly. Suzanne's gaze shot to the large bed a short distance away.

Oh, this is bad. Very, very bad.

Especially with how responsive she was to him. Anticipation was mounting by the moment—as was the fever in her blood. Putting her at a disadvantage. She silently cursed Leo for introducing her to sexual pleasures.

And what it was like to be this man's lover.

This was a situation perilously fraught with potential heartache for her.

Suzanne drew in a deep breath and let it out, then pulled her hand from his. Her skin tingled where he'd touched her. Distancing herself from Leo was so foreign to her, when for so long all she ever wanted was to draw near.

They'd been so close once, he felt like a piece of her.

And she'd carried on just fine without that piece for the last seven years. *Liar!* a small voice from deep inside her heart vehemently objected. She quashed the voice.

"What if someone is in need of medical care urgently? How in the world is anyone going to approach me—or Rolland—for help when you've caused pandemonium in the streets and in my establishment?"

"You underestimate me. I had my men visit every home, informing them about the contest, and what to do should they need medical attention. They were directed to come here to the inn and speak to Joseph. They would then be escorted immediately through the crowds, directly to you."

She blinked. "Oh." *Stop saying that. Say something else.* "I see…" *That was equally brilliant, Suzanne.*

Leo stepped forward.

She took an instinctive step back and came in contact with the door. He pressed his palms to the door just above her shoulders. The delicious scent of his soap and heat from his body instantly enveloped her.

"I think you are afraid of me."

She laughed. "I am certainly not afraid of you." Terrified was more accurate, of all that he was making her feel.

When there shouldn't be any connection between them anymore.

She slipped her hands behind her, pressing her palms to the door, to keep from reaching out and running her hands over his beautiful body. She was so sorely tempted…

"Then come with me. *Jésus-Christ.* How much more obvious do I have to make it that I'm still in love with you?"

Her heart lost a beat.

Tears suddenly welled up in Suzanne's eyes. A flood of unsettling emotions swamped her, shaking her to the core of her being. She began to tremble.

"*Please, don't…*" Were the only words she could push past the lump that formed in her throat. Barely an audible whisper.

"Don't what, *chérie?*"

"Don't toy with me. Not now. I can't survive another heart-spearing from Leo d'Ermart."

Gently, he rested his forehead against hers. "You'll never have to again. I've never stopped loving you. Not for a minute. I know I've said the words before. I meant them then. As I mean them now."

Her heart was pounding wildly. Hard, powerful thuds.

Oh God. What frightened her the most was that part of her, a small corner of her foolish heart, wanted to believe him. So badly.

He lifted his head, then cradled her cheek in his palm, her gaze captured in his beautiful eyes. "We are not the same people we once were, Suzanne. And the circumstances for us are different now. I want to make up for the past and forge something new. Better than before."

She clasped his wrist and should have pulled his hand away. But didn't. "How, Leo?"

"*Dieu*, it's good to hear you say my name again." He smiled. "You'll just have to come with me and see… Tell me you're ready to take a chance. We owe it to ourselves to take the gamble."

"It could cost me dearly," she said softly.

"It could cost us more if we don't try."

"You haven't as much to lose."

"I disagree with that statement. In losing you, I lost a lot. Something I don't wish to have happen again. Come home with me, Suzanne. You have family, people who care for you at Montbrison."

She blinked back more tears. His words wrapped tightly around her heart.

He gently brushed his thumb across her cheek, just as he'd done the other day. The delectable sensation shimmered over her nerve endings.

It felt as though she was drowning. Physical yearnings and soft feelings for this man pulling her under.

He stepped back and released her. The moment he broke contact, she felt immediately bereft. "What say you? You don't want to stay here and spend Christmas alone, do you?"

No, she didn't. The thought of it was abhorrent.

Leo watched Suzanne as she turned her head, clearly contemplating his invitation. She gave her ear an adorable little tug, then dropped her arm to her side. "Where can this possibly go between us? What future is there, Leo?"

He couldn't get enough of hearing his name from her lips. Soon, he'd have her screaming it in ecstasy. "You're going to come with me. We're going to see where this takes us."

He already knew where he wanted this to go. He wanted her to be his. Forever more. He'd sent Gilles to Montbrison at dawn to make sure everything would be in place when they arrived. He had a few surprises to delight his headstrong beauty.

And he couldn't wait to see her reaction.

"And if I refuse, do you have any more schemes planned?" she asked.

He grinned and crossed his arms. "Of course. It's what I think about at night: ways to get you to Montbrison. And the different ways I'm going to have you come for me."

For an instant, he saw raw interest flare in her eyes. His sac tightened. *Christ*, he had to have her soon. His body was so taut, he was ready to jump out of his skin.

She shook her head and looked down at the ground. A few ear tugs later: "All right. I'll return to Montbrison. I'll stay until Christmas and make perfumes for Elisabeth and Aurore. But nothing more."

"No."

Her delicate brows shot up. "*No?*"

"No." He took her by the elbow to the window of his room. "Your things are being packed as we speak. The crowd has been made to dissipate, just as my men were ordered to do once you entered the inn. My carriage is readied and on the street."

She looked out the window, then back at him, clearly surprised that his words were true.

Leo stepped behind her, slipped his arm around her waist and pulled her up against him. She softly gasped. The moment her soft little derrière came in contact with his hard, straining prick, he closed his eyes, and swallowed down his groan.

It felt so good to hold her against him.

He reveled in the pressure against his prick wedged against her warm bottom. It took everything he had to fight back the urge to roll his hips. His cock clamored for the friction. For her. His one and only Suzanne.

"Neither one of us is going to hold back while at Montbrison. To be clear, when we get there, you're all mine," he said in her ear, then nuzzled her neck, enjoying the sultry little sound that escaped her throat. "I'm after a complete surrender. Body and heart." He was so attuned to her, he could sense not just her arousal but each time tender feelings for him rose up inside her.

Feelings she was trying to quash.

Feelings he wanted to continue to foster.

"But first, beautiful Suzanne, we are going to relieve this agony we're both in. I know how to read your body. I know you're wet for me. I know your sweet little clit is in need of attention. And so are your perfect pink nipples. They're straining against your chemise for me, aren't they? I'm going to fuck you, then make love to you, then fuck you again. In that order."

She gave an excited little shiver. And it reverberated through him, all the way down to the tip of his cock. A dab of pre-come seeped from his prick.

"Leo…" Though it was uttered as an objection, a wonderfully weak one, he loved the breathless way it slipped past her lips.

"There's a surprise waiting for you across the street in your room. Go get it. And meet me at the carriage in one hour," he murmured in her ear. He'd been hard for days. If she didn't leave his room soon, he feared he'd break his promise and take her on the bed. Right now.

Reluctantly, he pulled away.

Taking her hand, he walked her to the door, and opened it. She stepped out into the corridor, looking as aroused as she was unsure.

"I don't know, Leo—"

"I haven't lied to you once since my return," he interjected, cutting off her words. Not wanting her fears to get in the way. "Trust in me… Just one more time, Suzanne. I promise you won't regret it. I have some surprises at Montbrison I think you will like." She looked so adorable standing there, even in that horrible dung-colored dress. Leaning in, he lightly bit that sweet little earlobe she'd been tugging, just to make her gasp.

"Go," he said, then closed the door.

There was quiet for a moment. He waited, silently willing her to go and do as he bid. Then, to his delight, the footsteps retreated from his doorway.

Only to rush back before there was knocking at his door again.

Frowning, unsure why she'd returned, Leo opened the door.

"What's the third reason?" she blurted.

He cocked a brow. *"Pardon?"*

"The third reason you came to Maillard. When you arrived, you said you'd come for three reasons. You told me what the first two were. But you never said a thing about the third reason.

What is it?"

It was obvious that this had been on her mind for some time. He couldn't help but smile. It proved *he'd* been on her mind. And that he mattered enough for this to niggle at her thoughts.

"Ah, yes. That important third reason. I neglected to mention it? *Truly?"*

"Yes!" The single word came out tinged with frustration.

"Well then, I'll have to tell you what it is." He paused for dramatic effect. "...At Montbrison."

Her mouth fell agape.

Leo shut the door, grinning.

CHAPTER SIX

SHE MADE HIM wait an hour and a half.

But it was worth it.

The moment he saw Suzanne exit her shop and approach he alighted from the carriage, to the roar of the crowd that had formed.

Leo's heart lost a beat.

Suzanne had donned the expensive deep blue cloak and matching blue taffeta-and-velvet gown he'd had placed in her room as a surprise gift. The winter wind blew back the heavy wool cloak, giving him a full, mouthwatering view of her décolletage, and the gorgeous curves of her breasts.

Her sweet form was so sumptuously detailed in the fitted gown. His cock turned hard as stone in an instant, despite the chill in the air.

She was going to be in tight proximity to him all the way to Montbrison. And he had to live up to that idiotic promise he'd made not to kiss her.

What was he thinking giving her the gown before they arrived at his château?

Merde. It was going to be a *long* ride home.

She stopped before him and looked around at the enthusiastic throng.

"You look exquisite," he said.

That brought her attention back to him. "Thank you." She

touched her skirts. "And thank you for the lovely gift. It is much more suitable attire to greet your family with." To his utter delight, she smiled. It was the first smile since his return. And there was even the slightest hint of that adorable dimple he'd missed so much. "Why are they all here?" she asked, indicating the chaotic crowd.

"To wish you a good trip. They're quite happy. I've given each some coin for their participation in the contest. A gift for the holiday." He wasn't certain how she'd receive the news, but he was being honest.

She surprised him with yet another smile. "That was very kind and generous of you. There are some in dire need."

Her compliment pleased him more than she could ever know.

It was pure joy seeing her brightened face, especially after the recent sadness she'd endured over the loss of her father. And he relished the moment.

"I'm glad you approve, *chérie*."

Briefly, she glanced at the crowd once more. "You are a force to contend with, Leo," she said, looking serious again. "But I want you to know that I am coming to Montbrison because I have decided that I wish to go. Not because you"—she poked him in the chest with her finger—"willed it."

The joviality of the crowd was contagious, for he felt happier than he had in years. In truth, despite the sexual frustration and living outdoors in the street, he'd been at his happiest this week.

He didn't give a whit what her reason was for coming home with him.

All that mattered was that she was giving him a chance to remind her how good they were together.

"You know, regardless of your efforts, and the fact that you've made certain they all knew that my father had been your family's esteemed physician, some will think I'm going to become your mistress at Montbrison."

It was his turn to smile. If all went well, she wasn't returning to Maillard. She'd be his bride. "Tsk, tsk, Suzanne. There you go underestimating me again."

"You have a plan to remedy this?" she asked, looking adorably skeptical.

"Of course."

"Do you care to share it?"

"Not yet."

"Well, since we are on the subject, I have given it much thought, and I have decided to give myself to you at Montbrison. Extensively." She stepped around him and climbed into the carriage before he could even assist.

Fuck. That practically stopped his heart. His greedy prick gave a hungry throb.

Leo ordered the driver to depart for Montbrison immediately, then climbed into the carriage and sat down across from her.

"Extensively?" he repeated, wanting to make sure he'd heard correctly. He could definitely fulfill that wish.

"Yes. I want a…" She looked down at her hands on her lap, for a moment. "Well, a reprieve from the sadness and grief. A small escape. We both know this won't lead to marriage, regardless of…any feelings we might have."

That was the closest she'd come to admitting her affections for him. His heart quickened. She had no idea what he had in store.

He was going to woo his dark-haired beauty senseless.

If after the queen's death, the king could choose a second wife who'd been born in a debtor's prison, no less, and have the realm bow at her feet, then Leo could pick a physician's brilliant daughter—who created incredible matchsticks—as his next duchesse. He might not be king, but his title was significant, his lands vast, his influence weighty.

And he had more fucking money than what was in the overextravagant king's coffers.

Suzanne simply couldn't fight it anymore. The carnal awareness practically crackled in the air between them. She knew he felt it, too. It was always there. She couldn't seem to extinguish it.

Not when he looked so good he made her ache. His dark hair and gorgeous light green eyes had always been a knee-weakening combination. And dressed in his black cloak and breeches, and a green justacorps—he looked breathtakingly regal. All this masculine beauty would be hers to touch and taste… Moisture seeped from her sex.

Oh, Suzanne, you are playing with fire. And she could be burned, worse than any injury her matchsticks could ever inflict.

While she paced around her room in Maillard, she'd fretted whether returning to Montbrison was a good idea. Or the most foolish thing she'd ever done.

Especially after Leo's declaration of affection.

And the feelings his words had rekindled.

She was intent on being cautious. On not falling madly in love with him again. She was determined to enjoy each moment of this sojourn. And not disquiet her mind with thoughts of the future. And whether Leo would be in it.

The one thing she'd learned from her father's death was that life can be snatched from you at any time. And she would seek whatever happiness she could get.

"Unlike you, I've not had the pleasure of carnal encounters since we parted," she said. "And I wish to enjoy your erotic skills once more."

Leo tilted his head. "Oh, I do intend to fuck you mindless, but no, I'll not agree to just sex. That is a ploy. One I know well. It is meant to allow you to remain at a safe distance—emotionally. I've already told you, I'm going after your heart, not just your body."

✶✶✶✶✶

WARM LIPS BRUSHED against hers. Then again. A soft silky stroke.

Suzanne sighed. Her eyes fluttered but didn't open. She was still so sleepy.

"It's morning, Suzanne," Leo murmured against her mouth.

"Open your eyes, *chère*. I'm not going to kiss you until you're fully awake."

Her eyes flew open. Leo was beside her, his arm around her shoulders. She looked around the moving carriage. Through the curtains that covered the windows, she could detect daylight.

Good Lord. It *was* morning.

"You've been asleep since yesterday afternoon. You never even woke up when we changed the horses," he gently teased.

Over twelve hours? Clearly, the numerous sleepless nights had caught up with her.

And it was no wonder. She woke up warmly cocooned in the corner of the carriage. In its lavish luxury. With Leo's solid, warm body against her.

Leaning in, he whispered in her ear, "What do you see out the window?"

Suzanne parted the curtains slightly and glanced out. The majestic iron gates of Montbrison, mere feet away.

Looking as beautiful as ever.

Like the gates of heaven… That was the very thought she'd had the first time she'd seen the tall, ornate gates as a child from one of the d'Ermarts' costly carriages.

While holding her father's hand.

Her throat tightened, a barrage of emotions inundating her. There was joy; she never thought she'd see her beloved childhood home again. There was sadness—an engulfing, utterly suffocating wave—for her father wasn't with her this time.

Nor would he ever be again. Not on this side of the stars.

She didn't want to be sad anymore. Even if it was just for a moment or two. And she knew Leo had the touch of magic she needed.

The gates opened, and the carriage rode on through. Leo captured her chin. "We're home. Now, you're mi—"

Fisting his cloak, Suzanne sat up and crushed her mouth to his, driving her tongue past his lips when he tried to speak. Oh God. He tasted so good. Better than good. The most delectable taste she'd ever known.

Her blood ignited.

Her kiss was famished and frenzied. She couldn't catch her breath, reveling in the delicious hunger and heat that he alone incited.

He shoved her back against the seat. Angling her head, he took command of the kiss, giving her long, luscious unhurried strokes of his tongue. Making her mind spin. Her sex responded with a warm gush. She couldn't keep to his languorous pace.

She needed more. Of him.

And this.

Leo broke the kiss, his heart pounding in his chest. "*Jésus-Christ…* I love your fire…" He was so fucking hard for this woman, his cock felt like heavy lead.

"I'm going to fuck you." His voice was rough with desire. "*Now.*"

It took at least twenty minutes from the gates of Montbrison to reach the château.

More than enough time to make her come for him. And take the edge off his own physical torture. He was already seeping spunk from the tip of his prick. He'd been at a cock-stand for too damned long. One orgasm—no matter how intense he knew it was going to be—wasn't going to begin to sate his need for his beautiful match girl.

"If you have any objections, voice them right now," he said, slipping his hand beneath her skirts with practiced ease. "Otherwise… I'm going to fill your pretty little cunt with my cock."

He skimmed a palm over her knee and up her thigh. Her knees were together, yet the moment she felt his fingers, her legs went lax and her knees parted. Leo smiled.

That was an indisputable invitation.

His sac was full. His body was rioting for release. But he wanted to hear the words from her mouth first.

Leo cupped her sex through her caleçons. She jumped with a sweet little gasp. The drawers were slick with her essence. His heart hammered harder.

"What say you, Suzanne? Is this mine?" He slid two fingers past the slit and sank them into her soft, wet sex. She mewed and jerked her hips up. A purely sensuous response she couldn't control. He groaned. She was squeezing his fingers with the most mind-numbing clench.

He had to have her soon. Or lose his fucking mind.

He began caressing her cunt, sliding his fingers in and out of her slick core with even, measured strokes meant to feed her fever, yet not let her come. "I'm afraid I'm going to have to hear you say the words, *chère*." Her eyes were closed and she was arching her back, trying to press her little clit against the heel of his palm. He easily evaded her attempts to rub herself against his hand, refusing to let her come this way. After all this waiting, he was going to feel her come on his cock.

She bit her lip and thrust her hips at him more insistently. Lost in the sensations in her sex.

Paying little attention to his request.

Leo curled his buried fingers and stroked over that ultrasensitive sweet spot inside her vaginal wall. Her eyes flew open. A sharp cry of pleasure burst from her lips, the sensation strong.

That got her attention.

He dealt a second, far softer stroke, just to hear her gasp. "Is this mine?" he prompted as he continued pumping his fingers in her perfect sheath.

"*Yes...* Hurry!" Each word said with breathless haste.

"Tell me what you want, beautiful Suzanne. Let me hear you say it." He stilled his fingers.

She whimpered in protest. "You! *Please...*"

That was a plea he couldn't deny. He was on the edge of his sanity. Leo withdrew his fingers and tore open his breeches. Freeing his leaden cock.

He was on his knees and between her legs in an instant, shoving her skirts up and out of the way. Then with a quick lift of her pretty derrière, he tore her drawers off, tossing them onto the seat.

"I'll purchase more later." He made no apologies. There were too many damned clothes between them. Gripping her hips, he hauled her bottom to the edge of the plush seat, and angled her hips for his possession. "This is going to be fast and hard."

She gave a vigorous squirm. "Too much talking!" She was panting. His breathing was no less affected.

Leo smiled at her fiery outburst, despite his state. Oh, he was going to give her exactly what she wanted. Before they reached the doors to his château, he was going to rock her body with a powerful orgasm. Tightening his hold on her hips, he held her still and wedged the head of his prick at her opening.

His groan eclipsed her soft moan. The crest of his cock was surrounded by the most irresistible heat. He couldn't wait a heartbeat longer.

Leo slammed into her, driving her bottom into the seat. She cried out, thrusting her hips up, sucking him in a fraction farther.

His eyes practically rolled back in his head at the raging pleasure engulfing him. Her grip on his cock was so tight, it was mind-melting, making his prick pulse.

"You're mine," he growled, then captured her mouth, possessing it with the thrust of his tongue. Relishing her taste. Her surrender was delicious.

He snaked an arm around her waist, and braced his other hand against the back of the seat, holding her in place as he drove his whole length into her again and again. Releasing all his pent up passion. He was in so deliciously deep, her inner muscles lightly quivering around him.

The sensations coursing along his cock were stunning.

She slipped her arms around his neck. Her fingers tangled in his hair. And those sultry sounds she made as she took each powerful plunge and exquisite drag only incited him more. She was kissing him with the most magnificent intensity.

"You want to come for me, don't you?" he growled against her mouth. "Just for me."

She was about to come. He could feel the contractions around his cock intensifying. He knew he was about to send her over the edge.

"Answer me, Suzanne. You don't want me to stop, do you?"

"NO," exploded from her lips. "Don't stop! I want to come…for you. Just you… Oh God, Leo. I can't stop it. I'm going to—It's happening!" She lurched sharply in his arms. He crushed her lips, muffling her cry with his mouth. Glorious spasms suddenly enveloped his thrusting cock, her sweet sheath pulsing and pulling around him, sucking at his shaft, in one spine-melting wave after another.

Semen surged in his sac. A bead of sweat rolled down his back, yet he fought back his release, not wanting this to end. Prolonging his possession. And his connection with this one and only woman.

She was his. His perfect soul mate. His true match.

He'd waited an eternity for this moment.

He rode through the luscious contractions until finally his willpower snapped and he felt the rush of hot come flooding down his cock. He reared just in time. Semen shot from him with intense force. Leo buried his face in the side of her neck and groaned long and hard as he purged his prick in a deep, draining rush that went on. And on. The final spurt tearing a growl from his throat.

Leaving his body shaken and his muscles lax.

Christ, this was soul-satisfying sex, the likes of which he'd never known with any other woman than her. His heart was still pounding and his breathing still quickened when he lifted his head and gazed into her big brown eyes.

She appeared just as shaken as he was by the intense experience.

That endearing little crinkle formed on her brow. "You said you'd be truthful… Is it always like this?"

Normally he didn't answer questions about past lovers, but he wanted to respond to this one. "No," he said honestly. "Not even close."

She smiled, moving him to one as well.

The carriage suddenly stopped.

Leo leaned in, and in her ear he said, "Welcome home."

CHAPTER SEVEN

"YOU LOOKED QUITE flushed. Are you certain you're all right, Suzanne?" Aurore asked, concern etched on her pretty face. She, like her sister, Elisabeth, and the rest of her siblings had green eyes and dark hair—like Leo.

But not nearly as vibrant and light as their eldest brother's disarming eyes.

The very man who'd set his mind on tormenting her from across the room.

In the most inflaming way.

"I'm fine. Thank you for your concern." She smiled. "Please continue. I want to hear more about Robert. I cannot wait to meet your new son."

In one of the four lavish drawing rooms at Montbrison, with Leo's two brothers, two sisters, and their husbands, the Marquis de Tabard and the Comte de Balbany, Suzanne was doing her best to ignore Leo. And his antics.

It wasn't working.

One would think it would be easy to become engrossed in the latest news from people she was so fond of. Leo's family had greeted her with such touching affection. As had the servants she'd missed and thought about these many years.

Yet, she found she simply couldn't keep her gaze in check— and not drift to the other side of the room, where Leo stood near the hearth with the men, brandies in hand, in conversation.

Leo had changed into a deep black-and-red justacorps, the knee-length coat making him look better than any man should ever look, if a woman were to keep her sanity.

And he had the uncanny ability to know when she was observing him—no matter how engrossed in conversation he seemed—every time.

Each time, he'd smile and stroke the length of his finger across his upper lip. Just under his nose. Her cheeks burned crimson the moment it dawned on her what he was doing.

Her scent was on his fingers, and he was making sure she knew that he was enjoying it. She felt a quickening in her belly. Her sex answered with a gush.

She tried hard to pay attention to Elisabeth and Aurore seated near her, but between Leo and the slight tenderness between her legs, she was being distracted repeatedly.

Each movement she made resulted in a small twinge between her thighs—a pleasing reminder of what had transpired in the carriage ride to Montbrison. Her insides still quaked in the aftermath. Her one night together with Leo seven years ago had been incomparable. Nothing in her life to that point had ever been as incredible.

Until earlier today. In his carriage. In his arms. She was having a difficult time keeping the memory and smiles at bay.

"Teething is a horrible thing. Our little Thomas had a terrible time of it," Suzanne vaguely heard Elisabeth say. "You have something to help a babe with that, don't you, Suzanne?"

"Excuse me, my ladies." Leo's voice yanked Suzanne completely out of her reverie. "Suzanne has been away from Montbrison for some time. There are some things I'd like to show her. We'll see you at dinner." He held out a hand to her. "If you please, Suzanne."

*****

LEO ESCORTED SUZANNE down the long corridor and was forced to stop. Yet again.

The servants were peeking from the servant stairwells and

corridors just to get a glimpse of Suzanne. She stopped for each and every one, throwing her arms around them in a warm embrace.

Not exactly the sort of thing he'd ever done with the servants.

Taking her by the elbow once she finished her greeting with Monique, the gardener's daughter, Leo brought Suzanne to the last door at the end of one of the many corridors on the main floor at Montbrison.

Opening it, he allowed her to precede him in, then closed the door behind him.

He watched as she took in the room that had been designed by Suzanne's father and built to his specifications many years ago. From the floor-to-ceiling windows making up most of the opposite wall, the winter storm that had finally set in could readily be seen.

The large snowflakes rushing past looked beautiful.

This was Richard Matchet's greenroom, filled with the botanicals he wanted at hand at all times, attached to the château so that he and his daughter could access the plants with ease. Long wooden tables ran the length of the room.

And there were massive blazing fires in the ornate hearths at each end of the greenroom.

By the time she met his gaze, tears had formed in her large almond-shaped eyes.

"This room has been kept the same since you and your father left," he said. "The temperature is always maintained as he wished it, for the benefit of the botanicals. The cook has been known to use the plants here for medicinal purposes, just as you and your father taught him. Whatever you need to make the perfumes should be here."

"Thank you." She had a smile on her face, but it was rueful. A tear slipped down her cheek. She quickly swiped it away before he could dry it for her. "He would have been pleased that you kept it so well."

Leo stepped closer to her. "I'm sorry I wasn't there for you when he died. I know little of the circumstances. What happened, *chérie?*" He'd always thought Richard to be invincible.

He'd healed so many people. He'd had a gift for medicine. It seemed inconceivable that he was gone.

Suzanne glanced down and absently traced a finger over the grain pattern of the wooden table next to her. Before she responded, he saw her swallow hard. "He wasn't feeling well one morning. By the time I returned from delivering one of my remedies, he'd collapsed on the floor... and was gone. There was nothing anyone could do." She shook her head. "I should never have left him...I never even got the chance to say good-bye." He saw two tears spill down her cheeks.

His heart broke.

Leo pulled her into his arms. She immediately circled her arms around his waist and drew closer. The gesture left him feeling as if warm nectar had just melted over his insides.

He rested his cheek against her head, her soft dark curls tickling his nose. "I'm sorry," was all he could say. Two utterly insufficient words that never took away the pain of anyone who'd lost a loved one. How he wished he had something truly consoling to offer. Her father had meant the world to her. And when it came to his daughter, there was nothing Richard Matchet would not have done for his only child. Including leaving the wealth and comforts of Montbrison—simply because he couldn't stand to see his daughter live brokenhearted here once Leo's betrothal had been announced and Suzanne had confided her feelings for him to her father. He had no idea how much Richard had known about Leo's night together with Suzanne.

And it didn't matter now.

Things were different. And he never wanted her brokenhearted again.

"Thank you for caring about him," she said in the softest voice. "It means more to me than words can express. And thank you for..."

"For what?"

"For bringing me here. I'm glad I came." Her smile melted

his heart.

He hoped that the surprises he had planned would bring her joy.

Especially the one planned for Christmas Eve. That was the largest, by far.

"Come, *chère*, I have something waiting for you I think you'll like. Very much." He couldn't help but smile.

*****

SUZANNE STOOD AT the door to Leo's private apartments that had once belonged to Leo's father, the former duc.

Anticipation gripped her.

Her every nerve ending sparked to life.

There could be only one reason Leo had brought her here. And it made her sex moisten. Her heart beat harder.

Leo pulled her in front of him, slipped an arm around her, and hauled her back against his hard body. A thrill streaked down her spine the moment she came in contact with his beautiful muscled form.

She squirmed.

"I brought you here for a delicious reason," he murmured hotly in her ear.

She couldn't suppress another eager squirm. It was becoming impossible to hold still. The ache between her legs grew fiercer by the moment.

"Really? I think I might I know what it is." This time he was either going to take his clothes off. Or she'd tear them from his body. She had to see all of him, feel his skin against hers.

Or lose her mind.

"Do you now?" He sounded amused. "And here I thought what I had planned might be new to you…"

Her heart lost a beat. Something new and wicked to experience with Leo?

The urge to fly through the double doors, yanking the tall, gorgeous, and far too sensuous Leo d'Ermart in with her, was barely repressible.

"Are you ready for your delectable surprise?" His warm breath tickled her ear. He was definitely grinning. She could hear it in his voice.

"Yes!" She was well aware how breathless she sounded. And she didn't care.

She needed him. *Now!*

"Excellent." He reached beyond her and threw open the doors.

Suzanne entered the opulent antechamber, with its frescos on the high ceiling, its elaborate wool and silk carpets and costly furnishings.

Taking a quick glance about the large sitting room, she spotted what she was looking for.

The door to his bedchamber.

It was ajar and to the right, just beyond the white-and-gold damask chairs near the crackling fire in the hearth.

Smiling, she started toward it.

"*Voilà.* Your surprise… *Iced cream.*" His voice came from the left side of the room.

That arrested her steps. She spun around.

She thought he was directly behind her. Yet Leo was standing on the opposite side of the grand antechamber.

"*Pardon?*"

He gestured at the table beside him. It was covered with rich table linen of red and gold. On it, silver bowls of various sizes. She caught sight of fruit preserves, breads, and cheese.

"*Iced cream?*" she repeated.

That was her *"delicious"* surprise?

"Were you expecting something else?" His lips twitched.

"I…well, I thought…" YES!

Amusement shone clearly in his green eyes. He rested his hands on his hips. "Come here," he said.

Briefly, she cast a longing glance toward his bedchamber, then approached him.

Leo slipped his fingers under her chin and tilted it up. Sublime little tingles raced from his warm touch all the way down to the tips of her breasts. "Did you think I was bringing you here to fuck you?" His lips twitched again, as though he were fighting back a smile.

"Uhm… The thought did cross my mind…"

He released her chin and placed his hands back on his hips. "Tsk, tsk, Suzanne. You wound me. Is that what you think of me? That my thoughts are of a carnal nature *only*?"

"Well, if you put it that way…" She shook her head no. "Yes."

He burst out laughing. "You are correct. And my carnal thoughts are centered solely on *you*." That made her stomach flutter wildly. "Now then, about the iced cream, have you ever had any?"

"No."

"Good. Iced desserts are a favorite of His Majesty, served at Versailles. It is absolutely delicious. I've asked our cook to gather fresh snow and ice to add to sweetened cream and create some—just for your enjoyment."

This was wonderfully novel, and she was moved by Leo's efforts to arrange this lovely surprise for her.

Trying to mute her base need, wanting to enjoy the lovely gesture, she smiled up at him, even though her entire body was still taut with desire. "Thank you, Leo. This is truly lovely. I can't wait to try it."

"There are two ways to best enjoy iced cream." He picked up a bottle that was in a large silver bowl, submerged in ice. "With champagne." He poured the bubbly liquid into a crystal goblet and waited a moment until it settled before dropping a spoonful of the iced cream into it.

It fizzed up but did not overflow. Lifting the goblet, he swirled around its contents until he looked satisfied.

Then he took her hand and walked her away from the food and drink, and paused at the head of the table at the opposite end.

"Here." Leo handed her the goblet of the champagne and iced cream.

She glanced down at it, then back at him. "What is the second best way to enjoy iced cream?"

The most sensuous smile tilted the corner of his mouth. He picked her up off her feet and set her bottom down on the edge of the table so fast, she squeaked in surprise. Yet managed not to spill her drink.

"Naked."

CHAPTER EIGHT

SUZANNE LOST HER breath. *Naked?*

She recognized that look in Leo's eyes. He meant it.

The light ache between her legs suddenly intensified. Her gaze dropped to his perfect mouth. She licked her lips, starved for a taste.

"Aren't you going to try your drink?" he asked.

"*Hmm?...Drink?*"

He smiled. "Yes, your champagne and iced cream." He brought the goblet she held in her hand up to her lips. "Taste it. Tell me what you think."

"I think I'd prefer to taste you instead."

"I'm glad to hear it. And you shall, in due time. Try the iced cream and champagne first. It's the only taste you're going to get. The rest will have melted by the time I'm through with you."

His words sent a hot rush through her blood. Quickly, she took a sip and let the cold sweet fluid slide down her throat.

"Well?" he prompted.

"It's delicious." It truly was. But she'd rather be enjoying Leo.

He pulled the goblet out of her hand and set it down on the table beside her. "It's been a very long time since I've tasted your pretty nipples. I remember how delicious they were. Open your bodice for me."

Suzanne's hands flew to her neckline and began opening the fastenings in haste. His words made her breasts feel achy. She couldn't stand having them confined any longer.

Leo watched, patient, the hunger in his eyes spiking her fever.

She struggled, her fingers fumbling. Upon arriving at Montbrison, she'd been shown to her rooms, where she'd washed, and with the help of one of the servants, changed into the fresh gown waiting for her. She was out of practice with the many fastenings found on such costly attire.

He pushed her hands away, pulled her off the table, and back onto her feet. "Let me," he said and stripped away her clothing with confident skill. Stopping to press hot kisses against her skin. Until he had her naked before him.

And her breathing was sharp and quick.

Leo took a step back, his gaze moving down her body in heated appreciation. She felt a heady rush.

He sat her back onto the table with ease. Then pressed her back onto the wooden surface. The table linen felt cool against her heated skin.

Leo placed his hands on her thighs. "Spread your legs. I want to see all of you."

Those blunt carnal things he said made her head spin. He was so sinfully delicious.

She complied with his request. Too on fire to be bashful in any way.

He skimmed his warm palms up her thighs. Stopping at the apex of her legs, he ran his thumbs over her wet folds, and opened her further.

She was so utterly exposed and vulnerable to him. Her sex wept.

"*Dieu*, you are so beautiful... Every inch of you," he breathed, scoring his thumb lightly along the slit of her sex. She gasped and curled her toes, mentally willing him to penetrate her with his hand. Desperate for some friction. Any friction from him at all.

"You are going to be *my* delicious dessert, Suzanne." His fingers slid inside her. She didn't know how many. But he was using just enough to create the perfect pressure, giving her inner walls scintillating strokes. She whimpered. "Are you sore?" he asked.

The slight twinge of discomfort melded with the pleasure and swamped her senses.

Oh God. "A little…"

"Do you want me to stop?"

"NO." Was he mad? She was dying with desire. The nub between her legs throbbed.

"Good. Now, back to those gorgeous nipples. So pink and pert…They need to be sucked." Without missing a stroke inside her sex, he reached for the crystal goblet and held it over her body.

She froze. He wasn't about to…

Leo tipped the goblet and splashed a drop of the cold liquid—directly on the sensitized tip of her breast.

She let out a soft cry.

Swooping in, he sucked her chilled nipple into his hot mouth. She arched up hard, a loud moan shot up her throat, her fingers tangling in his dark hair. The tantalizing pulls of his mouth drove her wild. She clenched down around his pumping fingers, unable to help herself, as they continued to slide in and out of her sex.

Leo lifted his head and swore. "I love your reactions." He plunged his fingers all the way in. The decadent sensation reverberated through her core, all the way up to her clit. Snatching her breath away. Her clitoris ached so strongly, it was unbearable. She raised her hips and tried to grind against his hand.

"No. Not yet," he gently admonished. "We mustn't neglect the other nipple."

She couldn't take anymore. He'd kept the strokes in her sheath purposely light. Feeding her fever. But not alleviating it.

"Leo…open your breeches and… *OH!…*" Cold champagne and iced cream splashed onto her other nipple. She bit down on her lip and squeezed her eyes shut, bracing for the thrill of his mouth.

It came swiftly.

His hot tongue and lips heated the cold tip of her breast, plying it with mind-melting licks and soft sucks, sending voluptuous sensations flooding through her body.

She shuddered.

Suddenly, his mouth was gone. And he'd stilled his fingers.

Her eyes flew open.

"Don't stop!" Good God. She was going to kill him. If she didn't die first. She'd never felt so out of control. So consumed with desire. "I need to…"

"Come? You will. But first you are going to learn how to hold it back. It makes for a stronger release. Place your hands on the edges of the table and be very still." He smiled. "And I'll let you come very, very hard."

She was so delirious with need, she quickly grabbed hold of the edges of the table on either side of her. Anything. As long as he got on with it!

The last thing she expected was for him to withdraw his fingers, set the goblet down beside her, and pull up a chair. Seating himself between her legs.

"*Jésus-Christ*. Look at you…" He spread her thighs wider still. "The beautiful Suzanne Matchet naked and wet on my table. A most mouthwatering fantasy."

He dipped his head, slid his tongue inside her. She clutched the edges of the table tighter. She felt his tongue withdraw, then, with a long, luscious lick, he lapped up her essence from her opening to her throbbing clit.

She jerked her hips upward with a cry.

"Oh, you taste better than my favorite iced dessert. If you want me to continue, you must stay still. Or I'll stop."

She was panting. "Leo, I haven't punched you since I was a child of ten. That will definitely change if you stop."

He chuckled softly. "Idle threats. Your lovely little clit is swollen with need. And so neglected. Shall we do something about it?"

FINALLY. "Yes!"

"Then be still." He slid his fingers back inside her, curling them and delivering a stroke directly over that ultrasensitive spot inside her vaginal walls. Her hips shot up off the table. He pressed his other hand down on her belly, pushing her bottom back onto the table.

"Be still…"

"I-I can't." He was pushing her beyond her limits.

"Yes, you can. You are going to have to trust me. And I will make it worth your while." He stroked the same sweet spot inside her sex. A soft, measured stroke. She stiffened with a whimper. The sensation was intense nonetheless. Yet, she managed to keep relatively still.

"Much better," he approved. "Now, let's give this sweet bud some much needed attention." He picked up the goblet.

Her heart lurched. "Leo… N—" Before she could voice an objection, he dripped a drop of chilled drink directly onto her heated clit. Her hips shot up. His hot mouth came down on the bud and sucked the droplet off. She screamed and shuddered.

Inside her sheath, his wicked fingers still tormented that spine-melting spot.

"That wasn't still," he admonished. "We'll try it again. Be still now."

She was shaking so violently, her body rioting for release, that being absolutely still was beyond her control.

Suzanne closed her eyes and braced herself for the next glorious assault on her senses. Another cold drop dripped onto her, followed by another hot suck of his mouth. She was teetering on the brink of a shattering orgasm. Each cold drip, pulling her back. Each silky suck shot her to the edge.

His name screamed in her head, or perhaps from her mouth.

The abrupt sound of the chair scraping backward startled her. Leo was standing. He'd set the goblet down on the table beside her.

The expression on his face had changed from desire to feral hunger.

"You've no idea what you fucking do to me. You belong with me," he said, then swept her up in his arms and stalked into his bedchamber.

He dropped her onto the bed. She landed with a small bounce.

Leo stripped off his clothing quickly and grabbed the base of his generous sex, giving it a slow stroke from root to tip. "*Jésus-Christ*, you make me so hard." Arousal quavered through her body. She had only a moment to take in his muscular form and his impressive shaft, before he sank a knee into the mattress between her legs, lowered himself onto her.

And drove his cock inside her with one solid thrust.

She moaned in approval. He was so hard and large. He felt incredible.

He claimed her mouth, his tongue driving past her lips. She threw her arms around him, their bodies molding so perfectly together. She felt completely possessed. For the first time in a long time, she felt complete.

And she rejoiced in it, her body taking each deep thrust and delicious drag of his solid length.

Driving away all the emptiness she'd felt.

Her release was imminent—every fiber of her being screaming for it. There was nothing she could do to halt the powerful orgasm that was surging inside, no matter how much she didn't want this perfect pleasure to end.

A large, hot wave slammed into her, vaulting her into ecstasy. She screamed, euphoria flooding through her. He drove in harder, ramming her repeatedly as Suzanne basked in the sublime sensations, her sex wildly pulsating around him, clutching and releasing his thrusting sex.

Leo suddenly reared.

He tossed his head back, eyes shut. A deep sound of pleasure rumbled from his chest as he spent himself between their bodies. In the grips of his release, the muscles in his neck and strong arms corded.

He never looked more beautiful.

His body finally relaxed. He buried his face in her hair, his breathing slowly returning to normal. Her body was still shaky.

She tightened her arms around him and held him, basking in a sense of deep contentment she hadn't known in years.

Seven years, to be exact.

Lifting his head, he gazed down at her, a slow smile forming on his lips. It was infectious. She couldn't help but return it. He brushed his lips against hers. "That was pure bliss."

She couldn't argue with that.

For the first time since her father died, she felt so light, she could fly.

"I love what you do to me," she told him.

His beautiful smile was unwavering. "It is what we do to each other that makes this so special."

"I don't think I will ever forget iced cream."

He grazed his lips along her jaw to her ear. "It never tasted as good as it did today." He pressed his warm lips to that sensitive spot under her ear.

Suzanne closed her eyes. Oh, the things he said and did. She was on dangerous ground. And she well knew it. Falling madly in love with Leo d'Ermart wasn't difficult—for any woman. Especially her. He was her one weakness. Tender emotions were welling inside her. And they were getting stronger by the moment, crushing her defenses into dust.

She needed a distraction. Quickly. When a thought came to her.

"Leo, what is the third reason?" she blurted.

He lifted his head, his brow furrowed. "*Pardon?*"

"You said you'd tell me what the third reason was for coming to see me in Maillard. What is it?"

He cocked a brow. "Do you really want to know?"

"Yes, of course." It had tormented her thoughts long enough.

"To thank you for your note."

Her brows shot up. "To thank me?" *That rude note?*

"Yes, I was rather flattered that after seven years, you couldn't resist mentioning my 'exalted posterior.'" He grinned.

She blinked.

Then burst out laughing. "*That* was the mysterious third reason?"

"It was. I thought it might get a rise out of you. And I like it when you're fiery." He dropped soft kisses along her shoulder, and she shivered.

Leo d'Ermart was too overpowering for her senses. And was perilously playing havoc with her heart. She had to protect the foolish thing.

Yet, he'd made no real mention of a future beyond Christmas Day. And she had to make sure her heart survived intact once this sojourn was over.

CHAPTER NINE

"DO YOU WISH me to pour the perfumes into the bottles?" Nicole asked. The daughter of the cook had kindly offered to help Suzanne with the perfumes in the greenroom.

It was Christmas Eve.

And Suzanne was a knot of emotions. She was anxious. Saddened. And more than a little confused by Leo.

She was possibly leaving—in a day.

And once again, the weather conditions were conspiring against her. Unseasonably warm days had melted away the snow. Then, late yesterday, a cold wind had swept in, hardening the ground.

Making it possible to travel back to Maillard. With ease.

After spending four glorious days and nights with Leo and his beloved family, in truth she didn't want to leave. She'd enjoyed every minute of her time with Leo's sisters and their children. Bouncing Elisabeth's son, two-year-old Thomas, the future Marquis de Tabard, on her knee, made her happy. And made her long for a child of her own—Leo's child—more than she could ever admit.

And then there was her time with Leo. *Pure magic.* More heaven than any one person had a right to on this side of the sun. If he wasn't whisking her off to make love to her, he was taking her for walks around the grounds of Montbrison, asking her questions about her matchsticks.

He'd always shown interest in her love of science in a way no man, besides her father, ever had.

This was the first day since Suzanne's arrival that she'd been free to make the perfumes she'd promised him for Elisabeth and Aurore. And she was having a difficult time focusing.

"*Suzanne?*"

Nicole's voice yanked her from her reverie. "Hmm?"

"Did you want me to pour the perfumes into the bottles?" Nicole repeated. About five years Suzanne's junior, Nicole's blonde hair and blue eyes were a sharp contrast to Suzanne's own dark coloring.

"Yes, please do." She smiled.

She couldn't make any sense of Leo. He'd said he loved her. He'd said he wasn't going to leave. And to trust him.

Yet, he spoke nothing, ABSOLUTELY NOTHING, about wanting her to remain in his life past Christmas day.

In any capacity.

What was she to make of that?

She didn't want to believe that he'd lied to her again. She didn't want to delude herself into thinking she meant more to him than she did. The sensible thing was to talk to him. She was running out of time to tell him what was on her mind. And in her heart. The plain, unarguable truth was—she was utterly in love with Leo d'Ermart.

She'd completely failed in guarding her heart. And she'd come to realize that she was incapable of having sex with him without soft emotions being involved.

It was already nightfall and Leo had been busy all day. Official matters relating to his duchy, he'd said. She needed to speak to him. Right now.

Before she lost her courage.

Suzanne yanked off the apron she'd donned and tossed it onto a table. "Nicole, I'll be back shortly."

If her time with Leo was done, then she intended to part from him with as much dignity as she could muster. She'd get through the heartbreak somehow. But she had to know…

Suzanne raced to Leo's study, her heart pounding the entire way.

Stopping in front of the door, she took a fortifying breath, then forced herself to knock.

Gilles, Leo's trusted man, answered the door, unbalancing her for a moment.

"Is the duc here?" she asked.

"Yes, but he is indisposed at the moment, I'm afraid."

Quickly, she stepped around Gilles, and found Leo seated at his desk.

"I need to speak to you." Dear God, he looked so devastating in his black-and-gold justacorps. She wondered how many lifetimes it would take for her to stop loving this man. Why did he have to be so perfect and so out of reach?

He rose. "I'm afraid I can't at the moment." He walked around his desk and toward the door. "We'll talk later, Suzanne."

She watched as Gilles open the door wide to allow Leo to walk through first.

"I cannot be your mistress," she blurted out. Surprising herself.

Not to mention Leo.

He arrested his steps, turned and jerked his chin at Gilles, a silent command for the man to leave.

Gilles immediately complied, closing the door behind him.

"You were saying?" Leo prompted. His features were schooled. She couldn't read much into his question.

"I… I, well…" She swallowed, flustered, and tried again, her cheeks flushed with embarrassment. At the moment, she wished she were a poet rather than a scientist. They were far better at flowery declarations of affection, than she. "I just wanted you to know that I don't want to be your mistress—not that you ever asked me to remain as such. But… But we never truly discussed the future…" How pathetic was she? She was utterly bumbling this, while every fiber of her being hoped that Leo would have something miraculous to say that would alter her plan for leaving Montbrison. "I-I wanted you to know how I…my thoughts."

Perfect. She sounded like a rambling idiot. So much for leaving with dignity.

He said nothing. His expression still gave away nothing. Uneasy, she shifted her weight from one foot to the other, trying not to fidget, then tugged on her ear once before dropping her arm to her side and smoothing her skirts.

She couldn't have made this any more awkward if she had planned it. At this point, she had nothing to lose. She might as well speak the rest.

"I will not deny how happy you make me. How much joy I feel with you. And that I-I… Rather… I love you." There. She'd said it. "I will be forever grateful that I have known you, as in knowing you, I have known what it is to feel true bliss. But I cannot be your mistress, if that is what you were perhaps considering. I cannot exist on the fringes of your life while you marry and sire children with another."

He crossed his arms and tilted his head. For an instant, she thought she saw a ghost of a smile. But it was so fleeting, she wasn't certain it had been there at all.

"There you go, underestimating me again," was all he said.

And with that, he simply turned on his heel and walked out.

*****

THE HOUR WAS midnight.

Suzanne made her way to the Grand Salon in Montbrison, Leo's note in hand. He'd had the note sent to her chambers, requesting that she meet him in the large elaborate room.

She'd no idea why. And after the disastrous conversation she'd had with him, she wasn't certain she wanted to find out.

Part of her was she was still irritated with him for his ambiguous response. It wasn't easy for her to bare her emotions like that—no matter how clumsily done. Didn't he realize that?

He could have been more forthcoming. As things stood, she was still leaving soon.

Her spirits were low by the time she reached the door to the Grand Salon, the room that was used for balls and masquerades.

Surprised, Suzanne was greeted by Nicole, who'd clearly been waiting for her.

"Good evening." Nicole smiled.

She forced a look of gladness she didn't feel. Each minute brought her closer to the moment she'd have to leave her home, Montbrison. For good. "Good evening, Nicole."

Nicole handed her a set of Suzanne's own matchsticks, surprising her yet again. "The duc has requested that upon entering the Grand Salon, you are to light the matchsticks and walk to your left six paces."

She blinked. The hour was late. *Six paces?* "What on earth is happening, Nicole?"

"I'm afraid I cannot say." She stepped away from the door and opened it for Suzanne. Inside the massive room, it was pitch dark. Just a blanket of blackness where she couldn't see a thing.

What was Leo up to?

Suzanne stepped in. The door closed behind her, enveloping her in the dark. She struck the matches, and turned left. In six paces, she saw a table emerge from the darkness. The moment she reached it, her matchsticks burned out. But she'd seen another set of matchsticks and a candle on the table.

She reached for it in the darkness, grasped her matchsticks, and lit the candle.

Before her, basking in the orange hue of the candlelight, was a stunning table, fully dressed with elaborate table linen, crystal bowls, and gold service. A table set for a number of people.

And on the table was a simple note, written in Leo's familiar hand. It said, *A feast for later. Ignite the matchsticks and walk ten paces toward the center of the room.*

Clearly, Leo had obtained the matchsticks from her rooms. Curiosity over what Leo was about gripped her.

She complied, and then came upon another table. She lit the candle on it and took a closer look at the parchments covering the surface. They were architectural drawings of a building.

When she picked up the note on the table, it read, *A new school of medicine to be built in honor of Richard Matchet, for those physicians who would like to follow in the footsteps of greatness. His beautiful daughter, a welcome teacher, whenever she chooses to share her bright mind and medical knowledge.* The handwriting unquestionably belonged to Leo.

A lump formed in her throat.

This was beyond generous and something her father would have been thrilled by. And she'd be a teacher in her father's school... "Turn around and strike another matchstick." Leo's voice made her jump.

She spun around and found herself staring into darkness. Grabbing another set found on the table, she ignited them.

Matchsticks suddenly burst into flames all around the perimeter of the Grand Salon, as servants illuminated the large room by lighting the candles on the tall silver torchères.

It was then she saw that Leo stood in the far corner, his family seated behind him. And they smiled. Large happy smiles.

She approached, a thousand questions whirling in her head.

"Suzanne Matchet, I do not want you as my mistress," he announced out loud.

Her gaze shot out beyond his shoulder at his family. Her cheeks flushed instantly. She had not expected that out of his mouth before his family.

What in Heaven's name was he doing?

"I do not want you to live on the fringes of my life," he continued. "Years ago, I was forced to rearrange my life without you. I don't wish to do that anymore. You are the woman I was born to love. And I..." He lowered himself onto one knee before her. Her heart lost a beat. She began to tremble as she realized what he was about to do. "...I am the man you were meant to marry."

Tears rushed to her eyes. His cherished face blurred just before her tears began to spill down her cheeks.

A smile tilted the corner of his mouth. "I want to give you the world. Lay it at your feet."

Oh God. This was a dream.

One she didn't want to awaken from. Ever. It was too good to be true.

"And what…what do I give in turn?" she asked, her voice cracking with emotion. He was wealthy beyond measure. She had no inheritance or dowry.

His smile grew. He rose and approached. Stopping before her, he slipped his fingers under her chin. "Simply *you*. To me, you are my world."

She was shaking now. "You did all this for me?" Reeling, she gestured around the room.

He gave a nod. "It kept me busy most of today, especially with my meeting with the architect." He ran his knuckles along her cheek. "What say you? Will you marry me?"

Her smile must have been enormous. She flung her arms around the only man she had ever loved. The one made just for her. "Yes! I love you… I always have." More tears of joy spilled from her eyes.

Applause thundered in the room from the many servants and Leo's family.

Her soon-to-be family. This was the best Christmas Day of her life. She couldn't shake the feeling of her father's presence around her. And she knew Leo had planned the elaborate celebratory dinner waiting in the corner of the room, the medical school, and the proposal for this very day.

To replace the heartbreak that came on Christmas Day seven years ago with a cherished memory she would never forget.

And she adored him for it.

Leo cupped her face and smiled. "And I love you. You are my favorite holiday present. I promise to provide you with champagne and iced cream any time you'd like. And I will love you until the stars burn out." Then he kissed her, softly. Sweetly. Full of promise, passion, and everlasting love.

EPILOGUE

IT WAS ON a wintery New Year's Eve they say when the Duc de Mont-Marly married his beloved Suzanne Matchet. Not in a quiet chapel in the country, as you may think.

But in the great city of Paris, for all to see, from princes to paupers.

By the next Christmas, they had joyfully welcomed a baby boy, who grew to have his father's dark hair and wickedly beautiful light green eyes. They called him Nicolas.

Just as the duc willed it, nobility accepted his duchesse. Though her title commanded respect, it was her bright mind, wit, and disposition that won their hearts.

Just as she'd won the heart of the most celebrated rake in the realm.

All the prestigious salons in the city enthusiastically welcomed her, where the intellectual elite—aristos, poets, and scientists, grammarians, writers, and philosophers—gathered to discuss and debate science and art, philosophy and books. All were impressed with the duchesse's repertoire of knowledge— while the Duc of Mont-Marly looked on with pride.

And so it has been said that there was an irony to this romantic tale between these two lovers whose destiny was written in the stars.

You see, the Duc and Duchesse de Mont-Marly didn't need those matchsticks to warm their home, or light up their lives. In fact, over time, the matchsticks were quite forgotten.

Theirs was a love that burned bright, and spanned decades. And they lived happily ever after...

GLOSSARY

Antechamber	The sitting room in a lord's or lady's private apartments (chambers).
Caleçons	Drawers/underwear.
Chambers	Another word for private apartments. A lord's or lady's chambers consisted of a bedroom, a sitting room, a bathroom, and a *cabinet* (office). Some chambers were bigger and more elaborate than others. Some *cabinets* were so large, they were used for private meetings.
Chère	*Dear one.* (*French* endearment for a woman, *cher* for a man).
Chérie	Darling or cherished one. (French endearment for a woman, *chéri* for a man).
Comte	Count.
Comtesse	Countess.
Dieu	*God.*
Duc	Duke.
Duchesse	Duchess.
Hôtel/Château	The upper class and the wealthy bourgeois (middle class) often had a mansion in Paris (*hôtel*) in addition to their palatial country estates (*château*).

Justacorps	A fitted knee-length coat, worn over a man's vest and breeches.
Ma belle	*My beauty. (French endearment* for a woman)
Merde	*Shit.*

THANK YOU for reading THE DUKE'S MATCH GIRL!

Want my next release for just **99¢?** Sign up for my **99¢ New Release Alert** newsletter at www.LilaDiPasqua.com. Each new release will be just **99¢** for a SHORT time only. Get notified. Don't miss out!

FIERY TALES SERIES

Novellas
Sleeping Beau
Little Red Writing
Bewitching in Boots
The Marquis's New Clothes
The Lovely Duckling
The Princess and the
Diamonds

Holiday Novella
The Duke's Match Girl

Anthologies
Awakened by a Kiss
The Princess in His Bed

Full-length novels
A Midnight Dance
Undone
Three Reckless Wishes

Lila DiPasqua is a *USA TODAY* bestselling author of historical romance with heat. She lives with her husband, three children and two rescued dogs and is a firm believer in the happily-ever-after. You can connect with her on Facebook, Twitter, Instagram, and Goodreads!

READ AN EXCERPT OF
SLEEPING BEAU

Inspired by the tale of Sleeping Beauty—an erotically charged historical romance novella from the acclaimed Fiery Tales series. One sleeping rake, one scorching kiss, one night of unforgettable passion...

Five years ago, the notorious rake, Adrien d'Aspe, Marquis de Beaulain, was awakened by a sensuous kiss–and experienced a night of raw ecstasy that was branded into his memory.

Years later, he spots his mysterious seductress–and this time, he has no intention of letting her go...

SLEEPING BEAU

Moral of the Story of Sleeping Beauty:
To wait so long,
To want a man refined and strong,
Is not at all uncommon.
But: rare it is a hundred years to wait.
Indeed there is no woman
Today so patient for a mate.
Our tale was meant to show
That when marriage is deferred,
It is no less blissful than those of which you've heard.
Nothing's lost after a century or so.
And yet, for lovers whose ardor
Cannot be controlled and marry out of passion,
I don't have the heart their act to deplore
Or to preach a moral lesson.

Charles Perrault (1628–1703)

CHAPTER ONE

France, 1685

"WILL YOU DO it, Adrien? Say yes. You simply must. I'm your *sister."* Charlotte's whine taxed Adrien's already thin patience.

Adrien Christophe d'Aspe de Bourbon, Marquis de Beaulain, stared out the window at the gardens below. Lords and ladies milled about, clustering near the fountains and along the pathways bordered by flowerbeds. His mood was foul. His audience with his father the root cause. It hadn't gone well. It never went well. Days after the fact, he was still irritable. He'd only just arrived at the Comtesse de Lamotte's château and already Charlotte had him wanting to leave. Her unexpected presence and the absurd scheme she'd devised had effectively soured his plans: a few days at Suzanne's abode, indulging in drink and debauchery to lift him out of his ill humor.

"You are my half-sister, Charlotte. We have *different* fathers," he replied bitterly. Raised in Paris at the Hôtel d'Aspe by his three uncles, Adrien had had all the male influence he'd needed. Or wanted. Except for the occasional horrid visit, his father had been absent from his life—that is, until a year ago when Adrien's mother had died. Since then Louis had injected himself into Adrien's world. Though Adrien wanted nothing to do with the man, his father was not someone he or anyone could simply ignore.

Charlotte rose from the settee and stopped beside him. "You needn't remind me of that. Your father is the King. At least he has legitimized you, given you title and lands—"

"He legitimized all his illegitimate children. Not just me. And it is a wonder there's any land left in the realm, given the multitude he sired. I doubt even he knows how many mistresses he's had." Their mother among the masses.

"Well, the Baron de Chambly still won't recognize me as his. He's never given me a moment's thought, much less wealth."

"Charlotte, *nothing* comes without a price." His tone dripped with disdain.

"Come now, Adrien. Enough of this. We are family. *I need you*." Her bottom lip was out in a full pout. "What I ask of you is not so strenuous. You and I both know you'll bed a woman or two here before the week is up. All I ask is that you bed Catherine de Villecourt as well. Charm her. Convince her that marriage is not what she wants. Lure her away from my Philbert. You're my only hope, Adrien. He's set to wed her in two weeks." Tears glistened in her hazel eyes. "I don't want to lose him. He's been so distant lately. I fear if he weds, I'll never get him back. She's younger than I. Fifteen years his junior." Two tears spilled down her cheeks. "He'll focus on his new bride and forget all about me."

Exasperated, Adrien let out a sharp breath. Charlotte and their mother were so alike. She, too, had harbored the illusion that she could accomplish the impossible: maintain her lover's interest indefinitely and remain his favorite for good.

"Charlotte, find yourself a new lover. You don't need Philbert de Baillet."

"Yes I do," she protested. "I love him! I don't want to live without him."

How many times had he heard those very words from his mother's mouth about his father? Love. It was highly overrated. He'd no idea why anyone would pursue it. Love caused suffering. Lust was much easier to deal with. And far more pleasurable.

Adrien was about to rebut when she added, "Look down there. There she is now. With our hostess."

Mildly curious about Charlotte's rival, he glanced down at the manicured grounds and spotted their hostess Suzanne de Lamotte. She was with a woman whose rich auburn hair looked a tad too familiar. He stared harder. From this distance, he couldn't make out enough details to be certain . . . but . . . The hair on the back of his neck stood on end. *Dieu*, it looked like *her*.

Could it possibly be . . . ?

Visions of the redhead naked in his bed materialized in his mind. He still remembered her face. Her scent—jasmine. And the sultry sounds she made each time she came. Their carnal encounter was like none he'd ever known. Perfect spine-melting passion. Her delectable mouth, her lush form, and her hot silky sex clasped snugly around his thrusting cock had him on fire the entire night.

In the morning, he was shocked to discover that she'd spiked his burgundy with an aphrodisiac. And she was gone. He'd been confused, a bit disoriented, and uncertain if the whole thing hadn't been a dream. But the scent of jasmine lingered on his skin.

And on the sheets, glaring back at him, was the stunning proof that he'd taken a *virgin*.

Furious that he'd been played, tricked, he'd questioned his friend Daniel, Marquis de Gallay, the host of the masquerade. Made discreet inquiries everywhere. No one knew who the auburn-haired seductress was. For the longest time he'd been unsure whether he'd be hauled to the altar or called out. But the lady's family never stepped forward.

She'd left him with a sizzling memory and unanswered questions. Worse and even more maddening, after all these years she still made appearances in every one of his erotic dreams.

Was it possible that after five years he'd found the mysterious beauty who had sneaked into his chambers and awakened him with a searing kiss?

Adrien stalked to the door, reaching it in an instant, and snatched it open.

"Well? Will you do it?" Charlotte called out. "Adrien? Where are you going?"

He crossed the threshold with purposeful strides.

*****

Moving through the gardens, Catherine walked arm in arm with Suzanne—her friend and former sister-in-law and the only good thing to come out of her brief scandal-ridden marriage. If Suzanne's guests were privy to gossip about Catherine's late husband, the Comte de Villecourt, they gave no indication of it.

Strains of music from the violins sweetened the summer air and blended with the trickling sounds of the fountains.

Her tension easing, Catherine was starting to enjoy herself. She'd remained in mourning two years—longer than her marriage had lasted—and had thereafter kept to herself at Château Villecourt, away from the gossipmongers who'd gleefully spread the sensational details leading to her late husband's fatal duel.

It was Suzanne who had convinced her to visit last year. It was Suzanne who'd introduced her to her present betrothed, Philbert, Comte de Baillet. And it was Suzanne who'd persuaded her to take this sojourn before her impending nuptials.

"You aren't really going to marry Baillet, that old bore, are you?" Suzanne asked, her hostess's smile affixed to her face as they moved past the guests.

Catherine's smile was genuine. "I am. I shall proudly be the Comtesse de Old Bore." Her laugh moved Suzanne to one as well.

Sobering, her friend remarked, "I know my brother made you suffer, Catherine. I only want your happiness."

Catherine arrested her steps. "I am happy. Philbert and I will get along fine." Philbert was not the most exciting of men, but she'd endured enough *excitement* to last a lifetime while married to Villecourt. Philbert was the right choice. She'd have a quiet existence, financial security, and that was enough to satisfy her. Shoving aside the twinge of regret, she silenced the small voice inside her heart that opposed the notion. It made no difference that he didn't love her. Or that she didn't love him. Such marriages were virtually unheard of. At least Philbert had enough regard for her to be discreet about any paramours he'd maintain.

Suzanne sighed. "I suppose . . . but . . . beneath that very proper exterior lies a vivacious woman. One desperate to get out. I fear the sheer dullness of the man will kill her."

"Suzanne—" Catherine's retort was interrupted.

"Madame de Lamotte!" a woman called out behind her. Turning, Catherine saw two women about her age briskly approaching.

"Ah, *Dieu* . . ." Suzanne murmured softly.

The two dark-haired females stopped before them, cheeks pink and slightly breathless.

"Is he here, madame? Has *le Beau* arrived?" blurted out Madame de Noisette the moment Suzanne had finished with the introductions.

"Yes, do tell," her friend Madame de Bussy, prompted.

"He is here." Suzanne's statement was weighty with a certain amount of smug pleasure.

Excitement bubbled out of the two women, the sound much like that of a gaggle of geese.

Catherine hid her amusement over their exuberant reactions. "Who is *le Beau*?" she inquired, her curiosity piqued.

Madame de Noisette's brown eyes widened. "You don't know *le Beau*?"

"I'm afraid I've never heard of him."

"Why, he's only the most handsome man in the realm," she explained. "He's one of the King's own bastard sons—Adrien, Marquis de Beaulain."

"And I hear he's between conquests," Madame de Bussy added. "His reputation as a master swordsman and"—she blushed—"in the boudoir is renowned. In fact, he's quite the celebrated libertine. All the women want him."

"Oh?" Catherine remarked, unimpressed.

Madame de Noisette tittered. "He's living up to the curse."

That grabbed Catherine's interest. *"Curse?"*

"Why, yes." Madame de Bussy looked around then stepped a little closer and continued *sotto voce*. "His mother was, for a time, the King's favorite. It is said that at le Beau's christening, one of the King's former favorites was overcome with jealousy, burst into the chapel, and cursed the child the moment the holy oil was placed upon his forehead."

Madame de Noisette shook her head. "Can you imagine such a thing?" Knowing how superstitious the King and his court were, Catherine understood the horror in the woman's tone. Uttering ill-intended words toward the babe was bad enough, but to hurl them at the anointing of the child was far worse. "Tell her what she said. Go on," Madame de Noisette urged her friend.

"Yes, of course . . . She said the babe would grow up to be exceptionally beautiful, charming, break women's hearts, as his father did, yet be *nothing but grief* to Louis. The King became instantly incensed at the woman. One of le Beau's godfathers, for his mother had three brothers and couldn't choose between them for such an honor, tried to mollify the King. As the story goes, he placed a hand upon the infant's crown and said that the child's looks and charm would indeed be great and that all would marvel at him. That he would fill His Majesty with pride, for a son so fine could only belong to the ruler himself."

Catherine glanced at Suzanne and caught her rolling her eyes.

"Really, madame, that tale has been retold too many times with too many variations to be believed," Suzanne said.

"It is true!" Madame de Bussy insisted, then turned to Catherine. "It's all come to pass. He most definitely has looks and charm, and at the age of majority, barely fifteen, he pricked his first woman."

Her friend laughed. "My dear, I believe you mean *he used his prick* for the first time to tumble a woman."

Madame de Bussy's face turned crimson again. "Ah, yes, yes, that is exactly what I mean. And he has been using that particular part of his anatomy to delight many fortunate females ever since." By the sparkle in her eyes, Catherine could tell Madame de Bussy was anxious to be his next conquest. Since most men preferred to live at their hôtels in Paris while their wives were banished to their country châteaus, the ladies before her could easily take a lover, as many did, without anyone being the wiser.

"And, my dear, let us not forget how often His Majesty has had to look the other way each time le Beau has broken his own father's law by duel—" Madame de Noisette's words froze on her tongue and her mouth fell agape as she stared beyond Catherine.

"It's him!" Madame de Bussy exclaimed.

Catherine was just about to turn around when Madame de Noisette grabbed her arm. "Don't! Don't turn around. He is looking this way and it will seem as though we are speaking about him."

"We are speaking about him, madame," Suzanne said blandly.

"Oh, my." Madame de Noisette removed her hand from Catherine's arm and pressed it to her bosom. "He is coming this way."

Suzanne was now facing her approaching guest with a welcoming smile.

Unable to resist a peek at the roué, Catherine peered over her shoulder. Her stomach dropped the moment her gaze locked on to a set of arresting green eyes. Sinfully seductive, intimately familiar light green eyes. Her limbs went cold and her knees felt suddenly weak.

Dear God, it's him . . .

"Hmmm? What did you say?" Suzanne asked, still focused on the ever-nearing le Beau.

"No, nothing." *Oh God. Oh God. Oh God. He's the bastard son of the King!* She'd tainted his wine with an aphrodisiac. He could have her arrested for that. For her rash—idiotic—act. Every fiber in her body screamed, *"Flee!"*

"Suzanne," she croaked out, her heart hammering.

Her friend dragged her gaze back to her, her smile instantly dissolving. "Catherine, are you all right? You're flushed."

"I've suddenly developed a terrible headache. I'm going to lie down. Excuse me." She fisted her skirts and made her way across the gardens, forcing herself to keep to a swift walk and not a full-out run. She maneuvered around the guests, never making eye contact, never turning around, using the bushes to shield her from le Beau's view whenever possible. Around the side of the château she'd find the servants' entrance.

Ten more feet and she'd be out of sight.

Her breaths were ragged.

Eight feet. *Hurry!*

How could Odette have been so mistaken? Her maid had told her that the beautiful stranger she'd spotted at the masquerade five years ago was a foreigner. From Vienna.

She rounded the side of the château. *At last . . .*

Tossing a quick glance over her shoulder, Catherine bolted for the wooden door, all but falling against it when she reached it. Briefly fumbling with the latch, she opened it, ducked inside, and raced through the kitchens, negotiating around each busy servant who got in her way, ignoring their curious looks. Smoke and the heavy scent of roasting meats assailed her nostrils and scorched her throat. *Move! Move! Get to your rooms!*

She rushed up the servants' darkened stairs and stopped at the door that led to the upstairs hallway. Cautiously, she opened it and peered out. Empty!

Only twenty feet remained between her and her chamber door. Wasting no time, she stepped into the long corridor and made her way to safety, her legs wobbly with each rapid step she took.

"Madame?" A male voice arrested her steps.

And her breathing.

She heard footsteps approaching.

Don't panic. It could be anyone. *Let it be anyone other than—* she turned. Her knees almost buckled.

Le Beau.

CPSIA information can be obtained
at www.ICGtesting.com
Printed in the USA
LVOW10s0850201116

513794LV00028B/781/P